THE HUMAN ABSTRACT

THE HUMAN ABSTRACT

George Mann

TELOS
.CO.UK

First published in England in 2004 by

TELOS
.CO.UK

Telos Publishing Ltd
61 Elgar Avenue, Tolworth, Surrey, KT5 9JP, England
www.telos.co.uk

Telos Publishing Ltd values feedback. Please e-mail us with any comments you may have about this book to:
feedback@telos.co.uk

ISBN: 1-903889-65-0 (paperback)
The Human Abstract © 2004 George Mann.

The moral rights of the author have been asserted.

Printed in India

1 2 3 4 5 6 7 8 9 10 11 12 13 14 15

British Library Cataloguing in Publication Data.
A catalogue record for this book is available from the British Library.

This book is sold subject to the condition that it shall not by way of trade or otherwise, be lent, resold, hired out or otherwise circulated without the publisher's prior written consent in any form of binding or cover other than that in which it is published and without a similar condition including this condition being imposed on the subsequent purchaser.

For Fiona and James, with love and respect.

'The broad mass of a nation ... will more easily fall victim to a big lie than to a small one.'
Adolf Hitler, Mein Kampf *(1925 Earth Standard), Vol. 1, Ch. 10*

Prologue

'And so the Children of the Earth fell down from the sky in a shimmering haze, their fragile forms encased in raindrops of steel and plastiform. The landscape for miles around was punctured and pummelled as they drove their way through the harsh Copernican atmosphere and punched craters in the soft loam beneath.

'The sky burned red with the trails of their failing engines.

'Slowly, steadily, legs began to unfurl from the drop pods that had survived, like petals falling open on the wind, and the machines crawled out of the ground like giant arachnids, their burdens encapsulated in bubbles of amniotic fluid deep within the safety of their metal forms.

'Later, these machines would go on to herald a new era in the evolution of the Copernican home-world, fabricating glittering cities upon its blasted surface and reforming the poisonous atmosphere around them as they worked. Soon water would lap gently at the shores of great settlements and the Children of Earth would discover the freedom of life outside their harsh, steel wombs.

'But for now, the machines would protect their charges in the only way they could, developing a symbiosis with the tiny foetuses that lived inside them, even whilst they sheltered their fragile human forms from the blighted atmosphere of their newly found homeland. These tiny children would come to learn everything from the machines; how to eat, breathe and copulate; ironically, these intelligence engines from Earth knew best how to survive the harsh lifestyle of a colonist. But for now, the reign of the machines had only just begun, and it would be many years before the first human form would taste the fresh air of Copernica and know it as his own.'

Excerpt from The History of the Copernicus Colonies *by Freiderik Roch (117 Copernica Standard), Vol. 1, Ch. 2*

One

'Books, like doors, were opened.'
Freiderik Roch, The History of the Copernicus Colonies *(117 Copernica Standard), Vol. 1, Ch. 27*

Memories decay, gradually, like words written in the condensation on a bathroom mirror or ribbons of smoke from the discarded stub of a spent cigarette. They dissolve into the cool streams of history and are lost, fragmented, on the oceans of time and space. Even the digital memories of machines have become fallible, or at least corruptible; the minds of men rebuilt in stacks of nano-weave remain, nevertheless, the minds of men, and as such are unreliable, self-absorbed.

Books however, books are something different, something entirely more vital. Whatever form they take – a valediction or a confession, a fiction or a history – they remain footprints or impressions, the graffiti of history, left behind by their authors to weather the years without complaint, to bide their time until they once again become relevant to a particular time or place. Books allow the dead to speak, and that, in itself, is perhaps their most valuable asset. For my part in this tale begins and ends with books, and that shall be my own valediction.

It was hot, the day Anna Hampton came to see me. The heat was cloying and humid, causing my collar to stick uncomfortably to the back of my neck. I had cracked the window open as wide as I could and was sat poring over the pages of an ancient edition of Roch's *The History of the Copernicus Colonies*, when the door burst open and Pharo walked in. I glanced around, reaching out instinctively for my cigarette, at the same time realising that I'd allowed it to burn down to a smouldering butt in the ashtray. I fidgeted awkwardly for a moment, and then reached into my pocket and drew out another.

'What do you want, Pharo? I'm busy.'

'We have a client, a lady, insisting that she has urgent business to discuss with you.' Pharo's distinctive voice had a texture that reminded me of walking on gravel, and a curt, clipped accent that betrayed his southerly roots to all but the casual listener.

I ran my fingers along the spine of the book, enjoying the tactility of the raised leather bands and the superbly tooled lettering and ornamentation.

A match flared briefly with a rasp as I ignited the end of my second cigarette.

'Tell her to make an appointment. I have work to do today.'

Pharo cleared his throat, embarrassed. 'I'm afraid she's really quite insistent. Her uncle has just died and she wants you to take care of the library.'

I folded the pages of the Roch carefully back into place, interested now. 'What was her name again?' The faint recollection of a news article or obituary was tickling at the back of my mind, insect-like.

'Anna something-or-other. Hanbry, Hamilton, something like that.'

'Hampton?' I ventured suspiciously.

'That's the one.'

I let out a slight whistle of recognition. 'In that case, you'd better send her in.'

I pushed the Roch carefully to one side of the desk and smoothed down my shirt with the palms of my hands, as Pharo stepped back out through the door that led onto the shop front. The light was slanting in through the crack in the window and casting dark, broad shadows across the corner of the desk and a wide expanse of the intricately-tiled floor. In the background I could hear the drone of the city, buzzing like the relentless hum of an insect.

I took a long, deep draw on my cigarette, and then pushed the remains of it into the ashtray, inadvertently dusting my fingers with powdery black ash. I wiped them clean on the edge of my seat, and then massaged the muscles around the base of my neck and shoulders, trying to rub some alertness back into my tired frame.

There was a brief chatter of conversation from the other room – a gentle, undulating murmur that I couldn't quite catch – and then the door swung open again and Anna Hampton strolled in.

She was obviously genengineered; the lines of her figure described a perfect waveform as she walked, which reminded me of nothing so much as a dolphin arcing gracefully through shallow water. It was beautiful to watch. I offered her my most charming smile and stood up, proffering my hand. She took it briskly and responded with a curt nod. I bade her to take a seat.

'Well, Mr Mihajlovic, I'm glad you've decided that you have time to see me.' The remark was biting, cold as snow. Anna Hampton certainly knew how to live up to her icy reputation.

'I apologise for the hastiness of my assistant, Miss Hampton,' I said, smiling genially. 'Please, let us begin again. Can I fix you a drink?'

She twisted her face into a visage of disgust.

'I think not. I'm here to discuss a small business matter that I want you to attend to.'

'Yes, I was most saddened at the news of your uncle's death

...' I studied her face in the hazy light, which cast mottling speckles across her cheek and picked out the dust motes that swirled, airborne, in the vacuous space between us. The family resemblance was uncanny; I'd chanced upon her father in a dusty auction house in Lecriox one winter, when in the midst of purchasing an ancient Solarian copy of Swift's *Gulliver's Travels* on behalf of a client. I recognised the close, chiselled features and proud aquiline nose of the father in the face of his daughter.

The Hamptons were descended from one of the earliest colonial families that had been established by the machines during the first stages of the colony. Time and experience had brought money, and money had bought respect. That, and the fact that Copernica's ruling class was composed almost entirely of similar genetic elitists who were descended from the original frozen embryos that the machines had brought with them from Earth. Like time itself, the human race perpetuated its traditions across light years.

I looked her up and down languorously, admiring the shapeliness of her legs underneath the thin veil of her black dress. Then, momentarily, I realised she was speaking.

'... a very sorry state of affairs. Of course,' she said suddenly, 'you realise that this is to go no further?' She looked distressed, startled, as if she had accidentally revealed a piece of information that she had been holding back in reserve, to use to her advantage at a later date. I nodded in a placatory manner, wishing that I'd been paying more attention. I'd have to get the shop AI to run a playback of the conversation later.

'There are twenty-seven books in his collection, most of them tatty old things that were imported from Solaria during the very early stages of the colony. I've had them all copied onto the house machine, of course – something my uncle should have done years ago – but I want you to find buyers for the original texts.' She hesitated. 'You do realise that I'm only parting with them because I have to? They've been a part of the family for centuries. Please ensure you get a good price.'

She was playing the role of the grieving niece well, but I was perceptive enough to hear the true emphasis of her statement – 'These books are worth a lot of money. Fail to get me a good price and the clients won't be the only ones paying.' I ran a hand cautiously across the unshaved bristles protruding rudely from my chin.

'I can call around and take a look tomorrow, if that suits you Miss Hampton?' I was already relishing the prospect of being able to handle some of the most ancient and unique books in existence, at least in the Copernica System; I knew the contents of the Hampton catalogue almost as well as the late bibliophile himself.

Anna Hampton shot me the sternest of looks, her eyes fluttering as she held her petulant temper in check. 'If that's the best you can do, it will have to suit.' She was already gathering herself together to leave, not unlike a small disturbance in the air currents that was biding its time, waiting for the opportunity to develop into a hurricane. 'I take it you know where to find me?'

'Of course.'

She inclined her head ever so slightly in acknowledgement; it is a worldly truth that old money craves recognition.

I placed my hands on the desk in front of me and raised myself slowly out of my seat. The texture of the light had changed, as if to signal the end of our conversation. The shadows now fell directly across the face of the enigmatic Anna Hampton, partially obscuring the expression on her face.

'Now, if you would please excuse me, I really do have a great deal of work to do today.'

She stood, smiling politely. 'In that case, I will bid you a good-day Mr Mihajlovic, and expect to see you at my uncle's estate at twelve o'clock tomorrow. Please be prompt.'

Now it was my turn to incline my head in amused agreement. 'Until tomorrow, then.'

And with that, she turned on her heel and left.

Behind her, the door caught momentarily open on the edge of its frame, and I could hear the intonation of Pharo's robust voice through the crack into the next room, deep in discussion with the shop AI. Then the door clicked back into place and I was alone again with my thoughts.

I reached into my pocket, pulled out another cigarette, and returned, distractedly, to my reading.

Two

> 'Seek not to question other than
> The books I leave behind.'
> Rudyard Kipling, The Appeal *(1940 Earth Standard)*

It is perhaps not unusual that meetings, that at the time appear frivolous or even trivial, later turn out to represent a pivotal point in a story, a true collision of personalities from which, with hindsight, one may reconstruct the beginning of a meaningful sequence of events. Time has a way of impressing on you the importance of a casual remark or a briefly-glimpsed expression or smile. Of course, looking back, it is obvious now that the part Anna Hampton played in this story was that of the fool, or at least the court jester: as unwise and unsteady on her feet as a child. But at the time of our meeting, I too was ignorant of the story that was beginning to unravel about us like the cold, entwined coils of a mysterious serpent.

I brought my aerofoil to a smooth stop outside the Hampton family estate in the early afternoon of the following day. As the engines were firing down and the skirts deflating with an asthmatic, gasping wheeze, I glanced at the holographic timer in the cockpit. Only five minutes late, but enough, I was sure, to make a point. I pressed my thumb onto the small pressure pad at the centre of the steering clasp to disable the controls, and then checked myself over in the mirror. I looked tired, dishevelled, like a man struggling to define himself in the throes of an overpowering addiction. I reached into my pocket and pulled out a cigarette, silently chastising myself with a cold, impartial stare. I turned away from the mirror as I brought a flame to the tip and took a long, rasping draw. I felt the medical nanomachines flooding my lungs like a cold compression, a tightness in the chest.

Allowing the smoke to plume out from my nostrils, I used the side of my fist to wipe away the smoky screen of condensation that had formed on the inside of the window. I could just make out the form of Anna Hampton, strolling casually along the herringbone pathway that jutted outwards from the great house like an enormous, elaborate runway. Sunken ornamental gardens fell away to each side of this construction, describing strange, organic patterns that defied further inspection.

I wound down the window, allowing smoke to billow out into the cool afternoon air. The shock of the cold was like a punch in the face, and I stifled a gasp as my body attempted to readjust itself to the sharp change in temperature. I dropped a sprinkling of ash out of the window and watched as it was dusted across the driveway in the dancing breeze; it would give the janitor rodents something to busy themselves with later on in the day.

I glanced up at Anna Hampton. She was standing about three metres away from the aerofoil, her hands on her hips, the long ringlets of her dark hair fluttering about in the breeze, as if they were tiny birds trying desperately to escape from the clutches of their mother's nest. I smiled and dropped the stub of my cigarette to the floor. It smouldered on the paving stones for a moment before fizzling out.

'You're late.'

It was a statement rather than an enquiry, a means of letting me know exactly what she thought about my lack of punctuality. I gazed at her steadily. Her expression was contrived to inform me that she wasn't prepared to waste any more time listening to my excuses. I didn't gratify her by trying.

'Yes.'

She glowered at me, and I could see that she was barely managing to contain her anger. 'Do not waste my time, Mr Mihajlovic. We're both busy people. I suggest that we dispense with the pleasantries and get straight on with the business in hand.'

I inclined my head in agreement and, after waiting for the window to glide neatly back into place, clambered slowly out of the aerofoil. For a moment the woman seemed to hesitate, unsure of herself, but then she turned about and began making her way back up to the old family house, her body swaying evenly from side to side as she walked. I followed behind her, purposefully maintaining a slow gait to offer me an opportunity to take in the grandiose nature of the surroundings.

Now that I had an uninterrupted view, I studied the building more closely. It was a great, gothic monolith, stabbing out of the ground, slab-like, to dominate the surrounding landscape entirely. Its dark grey walls were pitched and smooth, with programmed coral running across its fascia like a network of fractured white arteries and veins. It had been built many centuries ago by a swarm of advanced nanotech, in the days before the Slowship *Valperga* had arrived and delivered its unlikely cross-section of humanity to the colony, not unlike a bee that unwittingly brings pollen to a flower, enabling it to breed. It was not long after this that, with the swelling population, resources had become limited and the fabrication of such elaborate buildings had become wholly uneconomical. There remained, however, a clutch of such wonderful buildings peppered across the continent, the Hampton family residence being one of the finest, or at least one of the most well-maintained. I rubbed a hand across the stubble around my mouth and chin, pondering the view. There was an overwhelming sense of history in the air, a barely tangible reference to time and place, and I breathed it in, captivated and intrigued.

Anna Hampton, however, seemed to accept it all with the air of the over-familiar. She breezed hastily towards the entrance of the ancient building without ever wavering from her path: with not even a casual glance over her shoulder to ensure that I was following. I allowed her to gain a short distance ahead of me.

As I walked, I scanned the seemingly impenetrable gardens to either side of the walkway. Cleverly-shaped topiary created silhouettes that stood out proudly against the rest of the skyline; a horse, a bull, a carefully constructed and – I guessed – accurate portrayal of the Solar System. Earth and its Moon circled the old, swollen Sun in a static dance, as it had done for untold millennia. Once the mighty human empire had encapsulated all this and more. Now it was scattered across unknown light years of space and time like the lost fragments of a jigsaw that would never again fit together. I stopped for a moment to take it all in. And that was when I saw it.

The dominating feature of this elaborate, overgrown garden, the one part of the whole approach to the building that appeared not to exist solely to accentuate the age and grandeur of the house itself, was an enormous stone column that sat off to the far left amongst a patch of tangled bramble bushes. It rose sharply and pointedly into the sky, as if it were attempting to puncture the underside of the nearby clouds. It was decorated in a series of ornate pictograms or hieroglyphs, which, although I couldn't see them in any clear detail from where I was standing, appeared to relate a continuous story or sequence of events. It was utterly engaging.

I felt as much as heard Anna Hampton drawing up next to me whilst I stood peering at the massive artefact. When she spoke, I could hear the obvious amusement in her voice.

'Trajan's Column. One of my uncle's little extravagances. He had it reconstructed here about sixty years ago; a very ancient Roman monument that charts the tale of some warlord's victory over his mortal enemies.' She smiled when I glanced round at her, like an indulgent mother resigned to allowing her child to question her on a topic she knew almost nothing about. 'I think it reminded him of his heritage; I believe our genes were originally of Italian extraction.'

'I'd very much like to take a closer look.'

'Perhaps some other time. Today we have books to discuss.' She indicated with her hand. 'Please, they're through this way.' She paced the last few feet to the end of the path, then ducked her head under the low beam of the doorframe and slipped into the enveloping darkness inside. I took one final look at the column, almost tempted to slip away into the fairytale garden and examine it whilst I was momentarily alone, and then followed Anna Hampton into the gloomy interior of the old house.

Inside, the same baroque ornamentation that had been evidenced by the exterior of the house also filled the exquisite hallway. A grand, ornate staircase led upwards into further realms of dirty blackness, the spiralling, winding banister seemingly tamed from the numerous boughs of two great trees that erupted rudely from symmetrical holes in the ground. They had obviously been genetically manipulated; their uppermost branches wrapped themselves around the twin landings to form a great, organic barrier between the upper and lower floors. The skeletons of long-dead leaves were scattered, like snowflakes, across the lower steps of the stairwell. They looked as if they hadn't been disturbed for centuries. Indeed, for all its grandeur, the place looked abandoned, unused. Dust swirled about us in lazy circles as we moved.

My boots clicked and skittered on the lacquered granite floor as the grieving niece led me through the entrance hall and directly to the library.

It was a relatively small room, badly lit from a tiny, cracked window mounted opposite the door and dominated by a vast netscreen that filled the entirety of the south-facing wall. I guessed that the controlling AI had been decommissioned – or otherwise not informed of our arrival – as the flat, grey screen remained static and dead. I peered further into the murky corners of the room, trying to take it all in.

Clutter filled every nook and cranny. Archaic pots and plates, illustrated with bright, gaudy paintings of flowers and landscapes, were piled on top of one another on shelves that bowed dramatically under the weight. A table in the centre of the room had at some time been used to entertain; the places were impeccably set with an impressive array of cutlery, each item covered in a thick layer of dust. I picked up a fork, disturbing a mass of the greasy particles and sending them blooming up into the air, sprinkling my black jacket with tiny, light-grey speckles. I turned to Anna Hampton.

'I thought your uncle had lived here until he died?'

She looked at me strangely. 'As I told you the other day, he hadn't been near the place for nearly a month, and even then, it was only to plan his next expedition. Uncle Julian inhabited a very small number of rooms on the upper floor. He only ever came down here to tend to his beloved books. The estate has been suffering from a great deal of neglect over the last few years.'

I tried to remember the conversation from the previous day. I had no recollection of her mentioning anything about an expedition. I shrugged noncommittally and placed the fork back on the table.

'So, shall I take a look at this library?'

She offered me a half-smile, cocking her head slightly to one side, and then led the way across the room to a small writing desk in one corner, above which an elaborate case contained an array of spectacularly-bound books. I felt my spirits lifting. Anna Hampton leaned across the desk and carefully activated the thumbprint lock that adorned the edging of the ebony frame. The plastiform panel swung open with a gentle, pneumatic release, like an exhalation, or a quiet sigh of relief. I moved in closer and allowed my eyes to wander over the spines of the eclectic tomes, scanning the meticulously tooled titles that decorated them. It was perhaps the most satisfying, most mature collection that I had ever laid my eyes upon. Nearly all the important texts from the last eight hundred years were arrayed upon these two shelves; Jakob

Croft's *The Life of a Colonial Baron*, Isabella Cray's *Land of Antiquities*, Roger Graham Scott's *From Clay and Mud: A History of Humanity*, Jatinda Singh's *Children of the Four Horsemen*. They were all there. I reached out and allowed myself to touch them, trailing my fingers across their exquisite leather exteriors. I stopped when I came upon the book I had been searching for. This was the real gem of the collection, perhaps the rarest book of its kind anywhere in the Copernican System: a true first edition of Freiderik Roch's *The History of the Copernicus Colonies*, dated from 117, local standard. I slid the first volume out of its place, nestled amongst the other rarities in the old case, and leafed through its crisp, tactile pages. I breathed deeply and enjoyed the dry, musty odour. I could barely wait to get it back to my office to study it.

I turned to the woman who was standing to one side, watching me with cold eyes.

'My commission is ten percent of the final sale price, plus expenses. I can take the books away with me today, if that suits. I have a very secure unit back at the shop, and we're covered by a comprehensive insurance policy. I need to spend some time examining the items before I can construct a detailed catalogue.'

A slight twitch at one corner of her mouth belied her apparent amusement.

'Ten percent is a great deal of money, Mr Mihajlovic, given the size and scope of this collection. I was thinking more in terms of five.'

So, we were playing the game now, the centuries old dance between two adversaries locking horns over terms and conditions. I almost laughed out loud; I'd expected more from the icy Anna Hampton.

'Certainly no less than eight, I'm afraid.' I gestured towards the shelves of books with my arm. 'The inherent risks of dealing in such valuable items necessitate a high price. There are certain costs and security risks to be considered, not to mention a livelihood to be made …' I smiled in a conciliatory manner and steeled myself for her response. When it came, I was surprised by her capitulation.

'You drive a hard bargain, Mr Mihajlovic. Eight percent it is. And please do remove the books today. I'd like to get the ball rolling as quickly as possible.'

I nodded my agreement and tucked the Roch protectively underneath my arm. 'I'll start loading up the aerofoil. I should be out of your way within half an hour – unless there's anything else you need?'

'Not at all. Half an hour gives me just enough time to draw up our agreement with my personal AI. If you have no objections, I'll leave you to get on with it. I'll be found in the first reception room to the right of the entrance, if you need me. Please make sure you knock before you enter.'

I watched her as she strolled out into the dim light of the hallway, her heels clicking loudly on the hard granite floor.

I put the Roch down on the dusty table in front of me, and reached into my pocket. I was dying for a cigarette.

Three

'Adversity is the first path to truth.'
Lord George Byron, Don Juan *(1819-1824 Earth Standard)*

It is at this point that I should tell you I have seen the dead before.

No, more than that, I have seen death, watched as the dead have dissolved in the hungry maw of history, until they become nothing but fractured memories, fragments scattered on the breeze of too many years. Death is what teaches us to live and to embrace vibrancy, because when life is gone we exist only in the memories of others and in the words we commit to the page.

Anna Hampton knew death – it was in her eyes and in her manner, in the way she attacked the world as if it owed her an existence. And she would fight for this existence, whatever the consequences.

Lotte was much the same. She would sit for hours on a little hilltop near her home, examining the universe around her, toying with the ringlets of her beautiful chestnut hair. She would stare brightly at the empty sky, her clear blue eyes shimmering in the low light of the evening. For months, I was convinced that she was watching the constant comings and goings of the Scatterships, streaking through the night sky like tiny, distant fireflies, and I would sit there beside her, admiring the view. Much later I came to understand the truth, to realise that she was actually staring out into the open vista of space, looking for answers amongst the stars. I never did ask her whether she found them there.

It was later that afternoon, as I pushed open the door to the office with the edge of my boot and staggered in with an armful of old books, that I noticed Pharo had left me a note. I piled the books up carefully on the edge of my desk and picked up the card from on top of my workstation. The mid-afternoon sunlight was pouring in through the back window, puddling on the brick-coloured tiles and reflecting brightly off the glassy surface of the netscreen mounted on the opposite wall.

I spoke quietly to the shop AI, shielding my eyes. 'Afternoon, Spinoza. Could you opaque the window a little, please? I'm planning to do a bit of reading.'

In response, the light dipped marginally as an inky wash drizzled out between the closely-sandwiched sheets of plastiform, blotting out the worst of the glare. I opened Pharo's note and cast my eyes over the brief lines of neat copperplate inside.

Rehan
Popped out to meet Sara for lunch. Won't be back till late.
Speak in the morning.
Jonah

Brief but to the point. I smiled to myself, amused. I'd known Pharo for years, and he changed little; he revealed information on a strictly need-to-know basis. This was the first I had heard of Sara, and I looked forward to grilling him properly in the morning. He was certainly a dark horse.

I glanced at the tower of books balanced precariously on the edge of my desk, and, after hesitating for a moment, began slowly to take it apart. Carefully, I laid out the two volumes of the Roch by my workstation and heaved the rest of the pile into the safety of the storage case at the back of the room. After transferring the remaining books from the rear seat of the aerofoil, I sealed the case shut with a quick press of my palm against the smooth metallic panel of the locking mechanism. The unit had a low-level pseudo-intelligence and would seal itself hermetically, sustaining the perfect balance of humidity and temperature to protect the books from environmental harm, or vandalism. Theoretically, they could survive for centuries in its cool, protective environment without even the slightest hint of degradation.

I settled down at my desk in front of the Roch, telling the AI to screen my calls to avoid any unnecessary disturbances. I watched as the elfin-like image of its avatar receded into a pool of static, like a swimmer being enveloped by a sudden, towering wave.

I reached out and drew the first volume of the Roch towards me, flicking easily through the introductory pages. The paper was crisp and unspoiled, and the musty scent of ages-old print filled my nostrils with a dry dustiness. For a moment, I allowed myself to enjoy the tactility of holding the ancient tome, feeling its weight in my hands and admiring the quality of its binding. I could now count myself amongst only a handful of people who had been given the opportunity to handle the two volumes of this incredibly rare book.

I lit myself a cigarette, rocked back easily into the comfortable folds of my chair, and began to read.

My eyes trailed easily over the familiar words as I leafed through the opening chapter, Roch conjuring images of the violent geological history of the planet, with visions of clashing tectonic plates and vast, engulfing lava flows. At one time, the planet had been covered in massive oceans of ammonia, but now water lapped at the shores of impressive human settlements. Roch encompassed it all with his bold literary flourishes. I skipped ahead, searching out the beginning of chapter two and the magnificent description of the arrival of the machines. And that was when I noticed it.

Something was wrong.

My chair scraped against the tiles as I sprang out of my seat, grabbing my own, worn copy of the book from its place amongst the untidy shelves above my head. I leafed through to the relevant page and then laid the two editions out on the desk before me, side-by-side. I sucked deeply and urgently on the stub of my cigarette, drawing the unfiltered smoke down into my lungs, whilst my eyes scanned the two opening pages of the same chapter, line-by-line.

(i)

And so the Children of the Earth fell down from the sky in a shimmering haze, their fragile forms encased in raindrops of steel and plastiform. The landscape for miles around was punctured and pummelled as they drove their way through the harsh Copernican atmosphere and punched craters in the soft loam beneath.

The sky burned red with the trails of their failing engines.

Slowly, steadily, legs began to unfurl from the drop pods that had survived, like petals falling open on the wind, and the machines crawled out of the ground like giant arachnids, their burdens encapsulated in bubbles of amniotic fluid deep within the safety of their metal forms.

(ii)

And so the Children of the Earth fell down from the sky in a shimmering haze, their fragile forms encased in raindrops of steel and plastiform. The landscape for miles around was punctured and pummelled as they drove their way through the harsh Copernican atmosphere and punched craters in the soft loam beneath.

The sky burned red with the trails of their failing engines.

Slowly, steadily, legs began to unfurl from the drop pods that had survived, like petals falling open on the wind, and the machines crawled out of the ground like giant arachnids, their burdens encapsulated in bubbles of amniotic fluid deep within the safety of their metal forms.

The sky shone with a hazy dawn as human life began to spread across the new world, dominating the ancient planet like a rampant virus, the living machines fashioning their new civilisation from the very fabric of the world itself.

There it was.

The first edition contained an extra line, a sentence excised from my later edition. I stood for a moment, dumbfounded and confused. I read the line over again in my head. What was Roch referring to? And why the change? Lines do not just disappear from classic books between editions, even if they are centuries old. I knew nothing of any revisions that had been made to the text after the books' initial publication. What's more, it seemed unlike Roch to refer to our own race in such a negative light, likening us to a 'rampant virus'.

I stubbed my cigarette out in the overflowing ashtray on the corner of my desk, and then took a swig of water from a glass that I'd left there earlier that morning. It was tepid and did nothing to relieve the dryness in my mouth. I scanned the pages again, looking for other differences. There was nothing, except a small note with a number written in pencil at the foot of the page, either a page reference or footnote of some kind. I presumed the hand to be that of Julian Hampton. I flicked ahead to the relevant page in volume two and cast my eyes over the lines of text with some urgency. There were two short paragraphs neatly underlined in pencil. They read:

The constructions and conurbations of the early colonists now lie mostly in ruins, or else their material components have been recycled for use in the building of later, more permanent structures. Nevertheless, the archaeology of these buildings remains easy to decipher if one accounts for the immense influence of the intelligent machines (not only in the construction of the buildings but in their planning and design) and the tendency of the colonists to think in terms of simple algorithms and logic. This latter trait can be seen as a by-product of spending many years interfacing directly with the intelligence engines and using machine code as their main method of communication; the buildings of this era consequently reflect the formulaic conditioning of their architects' minds, and as such are basic, practical and unremarkable.

There do remain, however, a small number of early structures that have as yet proved too obscure to readily decipher. Given time, they may prove to shed further light on the skills and artistry of our colonial ancestors, but when seen contextually it seems more likely that they originate from an entirely different era altogether.

A further, oblique page reference was scratched lightly into the margin by the underlined text. I turned quickly to my own, one volume edition of the book and found the right page. The second paragraph was entirely missing; there was no reference whatsoever to the early structures mentioned in the first edition. A shiver of delight fingered the back of my neck and spine. I felt like a Policzia inspector who had accidentally stumbled across the scene of a murder, and was gripped by a clinging, morbid curiosity. Where would the trail lead next? And what, ultimately, was Roch referring to in the excised passages? I examined Hampton's neat lettering in the margin. It appeared to be referring to an entirely different work altogether. I grabbed for a pen and jotted a copy of the reference down on the back of Pharo's note. I tried to think laterally, working out the abbreviations in terms of Hampton's existing library. It had to refer to another book in the collection.

DS/R/342.

I strode over to the cabinet at the back of the room and perused the titles on the spines of the books. It leapt out at me almost immediately. *Dear Stone: A Gazetteer of Early Copernican Architecture* by Dr AC Roberts. I opened the case and slid the book out carefully. It was old and slightly tatty, and I worked with caution so as not to exacerbate the existing damage. I searched out the right page. It bore a line drawing of a tall, broken column stood alone in a clearing surrounded by dense forest. It reminded me profoundly of the very similar column I had seen earlier that day. I resolved to return to the Hampton house the next day to take a better look.

At the foot of the page was a small caption.

> *A fine example of early indigenous artwork, Column 12 22B can be found at the source of the Darlington river, high in the foothills of the Xian-Tatoo mountain range.*

I smiled to myself, entranced. A mystery was beginning to unfold, slowly and intriguingly.

I called up the AI, watched as its face re-emerged from the hazy wall of static on the netscreen. 'Spinoza, can you run a search for me? Key words are 'Roch' and 'virus.'' I waited anxiously for the response.

'I'm afraid that search returns a null, sir.'

'What, nothing at all?'

'Nothing at all, sir.'

'Okay, try cross-referencing Roch with Julian Hampton.'

'I have one article recorded sir, referring to Mr Hampton's purchase of a first edition of *The History of the Copernicus Colonies* twenty-seven years ago. Would you like me to produce a hard copy, sir?'

'No, thank you. Clear that. Can you try cross-referencing 'virus' with any articles referring to early Copernican history.'

A couple of seconds passed as the AI assembled and sorted the relevant information.

'There are six thousand, seven hundred and thirty-two articles referring explicitly to the White-Strikken virus that was brought to the colony onboard the Slowship *Valperga*, three hundred and eighty-two official articles referring to industrial accidents and twelve assorted articles that mention the common cold. The advent of nanotechnology all but eradicated the risk of viral contamination nearly a thousand years ago, sir.'

'Yes, yes, I understand all that. Just one more search I'd like to try. Can you find any reference at all to a number of passages that were excised from the early editions of *The History of the Copernicus Colonies* by Freiderik Roch?' I waited, unsure what I was going to find.

'I'm afraid that search returns a null, sir. Is there anything else I can do for you?'

I sighed, and fiddled with the matchbox in my pocket. 'No Spinoza, that's all for now, thanks.' The AI receded quickly from view. I turned my gaze to the window and looked out upon the shimmering cityscape beyond. The light had started to fade and the buzz of passing traffic was beginning to die down for the evening. I watched a few Scatterships drifting lazily across the horizon. This mystery was going to take longer to unravel than I'd imagined.

I glanced momentarily at the clock tattooed underneath the skin of my left arm. The mystery would have to wait – I was already late for my meeting with Lotte. I hurriedly pushed the books back into the cabinet at the back of my study and made hastily for the door.

Four

'Iacta alea est'
'The die is cast'
Julius Caesar (Suetonius), Lives of the Caesars, *'Divus Julius'*
section 32 (110 BC Earth Standard)

It is my belief that there is not a single human life that has not been irrevocably damaged in some way or another. In many ways it is this psychological scarring, this attraction to harm, that defines our abstract humanity and explains, if not justifies, our sometimes errant behaviour. Some, of course, are more damaged than others, and Lotte was one such; it was her propensity for psychological turbulence that initially attracted me to her. In those early days, I'd found it difficult to decide whether I wanted to wrap her up tightly in my arms and protect her from the world, or try to prise her open like a flower, or else make energetic and passionate love to her.

Lotte was a 'reboot': she had died in a horrific Scattership explosion nearly eighteen years earlier, somewhere over one of the polar icecaps, whilst she was taking part in an expedition to study genetic bio-diversity in the region. Her body had disintegrated almost immediately in the ensuing inferno, but luckily one of the automated machines called in to explore the wreckage had been able to separate and distinguish her DNA from that of the other passengers and had registered her death with the appropriate authorities. Lotte's parents had long ago had the foresight to set up a trust fund for their daughter, and it was this that had enabled the insurance company to order an immediate reboot. A new body had been cloned in a vat of thick amniotic gel, and a flash state image of her neural structure (which she had updated on an annual basis according to the terms of her policy) had been constructed and fed into the soup of nanoweave inside her head. She had been brought back to full consciousness only a month after her death, with a fresh body and an entirely new digital brain. Of course, she'd been able to remember nothing of the events that had occurred since the date of her last neural screening, nor had she any recollection of her traumatic demise. This gap in her head had become almost too much to bear. She'd developed an obsession, sorting out any reference to the Scattership explosion and the ensuing legal web-work of lawsuits and compensation claims. She had bribed officials at the local Policzia offices into giving her a copy of the recording that captured the final moments of the Scattership, and had sat for hours trying to separate her own screams from those of the other passengers. She continued to find it difficult to cope with the concept that she had died, and yet retained no notion of the transition into death, or had gleaned no further insight into the abstract states of 'afterlife' so long predicted by religion. She had retreated into long periods of meditation, when the machines inside her head would flit amongst each other at immense, inconceivable speeds, accelerating her consciousness until she would pass out, comatose, for days on end. During these times, she told me later, she'd discovered things about herself that she would never have imagined possible, and yet, none of it mattered, because the hole in her memory was a permanent scar that could never be satisfactorily healed.

Even now, she was still looking for answers.

The cool, air-conditioned ambience of Lotte's small apartment offered a refreshing respite from the oppressive afternoon heat and still, moist air outside.

The apartment was a single storey building formed out of great swathes of programmed coral, extruded from the ground in curving balustrades and soft, sweeping walls. It had a natural, organic look about it that, to my mind, always seemed somewhat at odds with the fact that it was constructed in a matter of hours by a highly evolved and specialised loom of nanotech.

I hurried in through the door, hours late, a cigarette dangling from the corner of my mouth and an apologetic phrase forming in the back of my mind, only to find Lotte curled up on the sofa asleep, her stockinged feet wedged underneath a pile of thick, red cushions. Her dark, syrupy hair fell in tangles in front of her face, spilling out across the arm of the sofa where she rested her head. I dropped my jacket across the back of a chair and made my way to the kitchen. I was feeling twitchy, anxious with the adrenaline buzz of having a new mystery to solve. It was this kind of literary hunt that had kept me in the book trade for so long, searching out old manuscripts and following oblique references in the hope that the talisman would be just around the corner. This time, I was sure I was onto something.

I stubbed the remains of the cigarette out on the edge of the sink and started fixing myself a drink. Moments later, I heard Lotte stirring in the other room. I made my way back through into the living space and sat myself down beside her.

'Hello sleepyhead.'

I slipped my arm around her shoulders, gently, and kissed her on top of her head. The scent of her hair filled my nostrils with fresh lavender. She blinked herself awake and then smiled up at me from behind several fronds of hair. Then she reached up and hooked a loose cascade of it with her finger, pushing it back behind her ear with a gesture I had watched a thousand times before. She was smiling brightly.

'Pharo keep you away with shop talk?'

'Not today – he's got himself a new lady friend. He went out to meet her for lunch. Said he wouldn't be back until late …' I raised my eyebrows in a gesture of resignation, and Lotte chuckled quietly under her breath.

'Well, I'll be. Jonah Pharo. It always is the quiet ones. You'll have to get the full details from him tomorrow so you can keep me up-to-date.'

'I will.'

'So, what did keep you then?' She reached up and cupped her hands around my face, brushing her palms gently across the roughness of my stubble-encrusted cheeks.

'Just business. Well, kind of. One of the old Hamptons has died and I'm taking care of his library. But there're a few surprises in there, a few things I wasn't expecting to see. Extra lines in a history book and sketches of ancient monuments I've never heard of. I'm not quite sure what to make of it all. Spinoza didn't seem to know anything about it.'

'Well, don't worry yourself with it now. You've got some making up to do.' She smiled coyly. 'You do realise how long I've been waiting for you to show up, don't you?' She leaned in towards me and pulled my face towards her own. We kissed, deeply, and then I submitted to her, kissing her face and hands as we gently and passionately made love on the sofa.

In the other room, the kettle boiled with a loud whistle, and was left to go cold once again, my mind on other things.

Afterwards, we huddled on the sofa together and talked about idle things; a new holodrama she had seen with an old friend, a trip she was planning to take to Keddleham in a few days, an old man she had happened upon in the street. I sat and listened to the soft intonations of her voice, the gentle lilt of her words as she whispered quietly in my ear. Her breath felt warm against my ear and cheek. Presently, we curled up together and went to sleep.

I woke in the night to the sound of screams. My eyes flicked open and I sat up with a start. Lotte was in the bedroom, listening to the recording of her Scattership crash. I held my breath and listened to the rattling drone of the failing engines and the horrified moans of people trying to come to terms with their own, imminent mortality. Their screaming echoed around the apartment in the enveloping darkness. I had heard those screams a thousand times before, but like a soldier who never grows used to the deafening cacophony of battle, I could never become comfortable in their presence. I closed my eyes and tried to blot out the noise.

When I woke again, I was still lying sprawled out on the sofa, my neck stiff from sleeping in an awkward posture, my eyes bleary in the morning light that was streaking in through the window in opalescent shafts. I rubbed powdery sleep away from my eyelids with the back of my hand, then found my jacket and rummaged around in the pockets, trying to search out a cigarette. Lotte hated me smoking in her apartment, but I guessed she had crashed out in the bedroom, as she was nowhere to be seen. Smoke formed lazy curlicues in the sunlight as I filled my lungs with a sharp draw. I rubbed my face in my hands to try and wake myself up. I could still smell Lotte on my fingers.

My head was still buzzing with questions about the Roch and its possible relationship to the drawing in the Roberts book. I needed to spend some time with the books themselves, digging around, and to take a proper look at the column in Julian Hampton's front garden. There had to be something obvious that I was missing.

I pulled my shirt on over my head and grabbed my jacket from the floor. A shower would have to wait for a while, and Lotte would know where to find me when she finally woke. I knew that I wouldn't be able to rest properly until I'd spent some time on my own, trying to look at the puzzle from a variety of different angles and examining the books more thoroughly for clues.

I looked in on Lotte just before I skipped out of the door. She was curled up underneath the covers on her bed, foetus-like, her knees tucked up to her chest and her hands clasped tightly together underneath her pillow. She looked just like a child: fragile, innocent and new to the world. But I knew life to be far more complicated than that, and so did Lotte. I blew her a kiss and then made my way out to the aerofoil, sealing the door shut behind me with a mechanical click.

The door to the shop was slightly ajar when I pulled the aerofoil to a stop on the walkway outside. It was still early, and there were very few people about; the empty streets seemed like the tired pathways of an ancient maze from which many of the contestants had finally escaped. I presumed Pharo had arrived early at the shop to open up.

I disabled the aerofoil controls with a quick punch to the steering clasp and climbed out, stretching my weary limbs. I massaged the muscles at the base of my neck, trying to rub out the dull ache from the night before.

As I approached the shop, I realised that the lights were still switched off. Pharo must have only just arrived. I strolled in, calling his name.

'Morning Jonah, it's me. I'll just drop my things upstairs and I'll be with you.'

There was no reply.

'Spinoza? Can you turn the lights up please? It's a little dark in here.'

Everything remained still, quiet and dark. I heard the low hum of an aerofoil passing by in the street outside.

I dropped my jacket on the counter and pushed my way through into the back room, the door creaking shut behind me with a low moan. The window threw a spectrum of mottled light across the desk and the bookshelves, illuminating the titles on a hundred reproduction spines. I allowed my eyes to focus in the dim light. A few years previously I'd purchased an off-the-shelf virus to rewrite the inner structure of my eyes, so I had no problem differentiating things in the low light; it helped enormously with the long periods of reading. I scanned around, looking for evidence that Pharo might have left me another note.

And that was when I saw him, lying dead on the floor.

His body was sprawled out, face down, on the cold tiles, surrounded by a coalescing pool of his own dark blood. His left hand had been severed at the wrist and it seemed as if he had bled out; his clothes were soaked through, and a thick, red puddle obscured the side of his face from view.

For a moment, I looked on with a calm detachment, my heart kicking loudly in my chest.

I knelt down beside him and pressed my hand against the soft, bristly skin around his throat. He was cold, clammy and rigid.

'Oh, Pharo ...'

I could feel the panic rising inside me like a flood. I glanced around the room, trying to reason with myself. Why would anyone do such a thing? And to Pharo, of all people? My eyes settled on the sealed bookcase at the back of the room. Blood was smeared across the palmprint lock, and what looked like the remains of Pharo's hand lay on the floor nearby, a waxy, fleshy spider that, to me, looked more like the broken component of a model than the severed body part of my old friend. I looked back to the bookcase. Everything was still intact – Pharo didn't have the necessary authorisation codes to access any of the really rare books. Nothing else appeared to have been touched. I tried to raise the AI again.

'Spinoza, what the fuck is going on? Spinoza?' I was practically screaming at the netscreen, yet it remained static, as dead as poor Pharo lying prone on the floor. He looked like a broken doll, his arms and legs splayed at angles they were never meant to achieve. It looked like he'd been beaten, violently and without constraint. His clothes were torn and the exposed expanse of his back looked badly bruised where he had obviously taken a number of blows. I turned around and vomited loudly, a stream of sour bile dribbling out across my chin. I wiped at it with the back of my hand, ineffectually. I felt dizzy, unreal, like any moment I was going to come to my senses and realise that I was still crashed out uncomfortably on the sofa in Lotte's apartment, participating in a particularly lucid and horrifying dream. But the bile tasted all too bitter and real in my mouth.

I stood up and fled into the street, frantically searching for the aerofoil where I could make use of the machine's AI to contact the Policzia.

Five

'There are words within words, just as there are secrets within people.'
Isabella Cray, Land of Antiquities *(68 Copernica Standard)*

On what level does the difference between a life and a death become truly meaningful? Do we assess a life only by the impressions that person has made on other lives, or are the quiet moments just as valid, the body of inaction that defines the majority of a person's existence? Is it fair to judge someone on the brief moments in which our lives have intersected, or should we take the whole of that person into account, understand that we shall never know the entire nature of our friends and loved ones? I have no answers to these persistent questions. And yet, in Pharo's case, I feel there is a certain justification in at least *asking* the questions, some act of retrospective moral judgment that still needs to be committed. Pharo did not leave much of himself in the world; his presence was light and unassuming, like the tiny footprint left behind by a bird in the snow, and his family were mostly dead or off-planet. His affects were personal and discreet, and, so far as I could find at the time, there were no diaries, address books or letters that would help to reveal the true nature of the man. Perhaps it is a difficult lesson to learn, but it is only when someone is gone that you realise how little about them you truly knew.

Of course, a reboot was out of the question. Aside from the financial implications – Pharo was not insured – I was told that he had never had a pattern imprint made of his brain, or at least had never had one officially registered with a rebirthing facility. His neural structure had decayed so rapidly in the intervening time between his fatal assault and the moment that I stumbled upon his body, that a post-mortem scan was entirely impracticable. I tell myself that, had it been possible, I would have found the means to help him. In truth, it is unlikely that I could have afforded to make a difference. But that is the nature of our own selfish absolution. We strive to free ourselves from the shackles of blame and responsibility. Yet, I continue to feel an acute spike of guilt when I consider that my actions played a fundamental part in the slow and agonising death of my oldest friend.

The room was busy with a million mechanical spiders. They crawled in swarms over every surface, their tiny metallic legs clacking against the tiled floor of the office and the tired wooden surface of my old desk. I watched them scampering amongst each other, stopping every now and then to examine some minute detail that I couldn't see, or to push one of their strange, phallic-looking proboscises into the orifice of another to transmit data and compile their vast ocean of information. Soon, I was told, they would have the entire room mapped out in all its atomic complexity.

They continued to scuttle around my feet, skidding out of the way every time I altered my posture and looked as if I was about to tread on one of them.

The Policzia had dusted the entire building with these tiny machines in an effort to gather information and build a virtugraphic image of the crime scene. The spiders themselves were operated by a subroutine of one of the main Policzia AIs, a very complex and chaotic form of hive mind. The AI itself stood in the corner of the room, surveying the scene. It had adopted a skeletal, humanoid frame in an effort to provide itself with some mobility, although to me it looked slightly skewed, unbalanced. Not to mention creepy.

In truth, it seemed the AIs were entirely capable of managing the whole investigation themselves, but as far as I could tell had consented to two human officers attending the scene, if only out of pity or a dubious sense of propriety.

Lotte was sat in the front of the building, smoking one of my cigarettes. She had come over shortly after the Policzia had arrived and I had called her to let her know what was going on. She was wrapped in a large, blue overcoat and hunched over her compad, scanning the channels for the morning news. She hadn't had time to dress properly before leaving her apartment and the previous night's make-up was still smudged around her eyes and mouth. I had stopped her from walking into my office and catching sight of Pharo's body, although I knew all too well that she had faced far worse in her own life. I imagined that her morbid preoccupation with her own death had long ago led her to sought out the archive images of her own obliterated body. I glanced around the doorframe at her with a quick smile. She sipped half-heartedly at a mug of stale coffee, and then waved when she noticed me looking. The smile on her face was tender, sad. I thought she was the most beautiful thing I had ever seen. All I wanted to do was get out of there, head back to Lotte's place and try to blot it all out for a while. Although I was sure that wasn't going to happen for at least another couple of hours.

I turned to one of the human inspectors who was dawdling beside me. Pharo's body was still lying in situ by our feet. I felt oddly detached, as if I was looking on at the scene from an omnipotent vantage point high above the room. I felt vaguely disgusted with myself for the fact that I was slowly growing accustomed to the sight of my friend's unmoving body on the office floor, continuously being violated by a series of silvery, mechanical spiders. They clustered around the stump of his severed hand like an army of soldier ants attracted to the sweet scent of sugar.

For me, everything was a little blurry around the edges. One of the four Policzia AIs that now patrolled the building had given me a sharp injection in my arm just after my interview, allegedly containing something that would help to calm me down. It had succeeded only in making me feel more nauseous than before.

The officer looked back at me glumly from underneath the rim of his hat.

'It's a long time since we've seen anything like this – murder-in-the-first-degree and all that. I don't know how they managed to scramble your AI, but they did a bloody good job of it. It's taking our boys a whole while to get it back up and running again.' He nodded in the direction of the netscreen, which remained devoid of any activity.

'Do you think you're going to be able to get them, though? Eventually, I mean?' I was still hopeful that Spinoza would be able to shed some light on what had happened.

'That all depends on whether your AI was able to record anything before it was screwed over. Personally I think the chances are pretty slim. The people who did this to your friend obviously knew what they were doing.'

One of the intelligence engines, another of the strange, skeletal constructs about the size of a dog, that skittered about on four blade-like legs and had a disturbing, featureless skull of silicone-composite mounted on its 'shoulders', swivelled about and trained its sensor array on the man standing next to me.

'Officer Tribauer, a word if I may?'

He shrugged his shoulders nonchalantly and stepped over Pharo's body, crouching down to place his ear near the mouthpiece of the AI's frame. His brow wrinkled into a frown as the machine spoke quietly into his ear. I saw his dark beard bristle as he mouthed something back, before he straightened his shoulders with a loud sigh and stepped backwards over Pharo's corpse to stand beside me once again. A little cluster of spiders dashed out of the way of his heavy boots.

'Sorry about that. Of course, we will do all we can to trace, arrest and prosecute Mr Pharo's assailant. It's just a matter of time before the AIs turn over some evidence from the room.' He glanced awkwardly at the strange, four-legged machine, which had now gone back to scanning the floor around the immediate vicinity of the corpse. 'At the moment we're assuming it was an attempted robbery that went wrong when Mr Pharo tried to intervene. And that means it has to be someone who knew about the expensive books ...' He indicated the sealed cabinet at the back of the room, still smeared with a large, greasy streak of congealed blood. 'If you can think of anyone else who may have heard about your recent acquisitions?' I couldn't.

'I presume you are going to speak to Miss Hampton?'

'Indeed, indeed. All in due course. For now we need to sit tight and wait ... aahhh. Looks like your AI is talking to us once again.'

I looked round at the netscreen on the wall. Images flickered by in quick succession; a face here, a shot of the room there. My face bloomed suddenly onto the screen, and then disappeared almost as quickly. Trying to focus on any of these images was like looking out of the window of a fast moving vehicle: glimpses and half-remembered impressions of movement made quick and slight stains on the back of my retina, only to be replaced a second later when the picture changed. I blinked, and tried to take in the scene. The AI in the corner – the one with the vaguely humanoid skeleton – was obviously communicating with Spinoza on some machine level, blinking thousands of machine code messages back and forth in the space it would take me to draw breath. I waited.

Presently, the deluge of activity stopped and the screen went blank once again. The AI swivelled its head around and turned its attention to the room. It had a strange, metallic edge to its voice when it finally spoke.

'There are no records that detail any occurrence in the building after 21:16 yesterday evening. The machine, known as Spinoza, appears to have been deactivated at that time by a magnetic pulse that scrambled a number of its fundamental neural circuits. These have now been restored in full. There are a number of other, prior records that may or may not be related to the case in hand.'

The other human officer stepped forward a little. 'Shall we review them anyway? It can't hurt to cover all the available information whilst we're here.'

The AI nodded its agreement. 'Indeed. I shall reset the timeframe by two days to Mr Mihajlovic's first encounter with Miss Hampton and their discussion regarding the sale of Julian Hampton's collection of books.' The image on the screen flickered briefly and then I could see myself sitting at the desk, watching Anna Hampton as she strolled confidently into the room. I saw myself stand to greet her, and then my words emanated from the direction of the netscreen.

'... I apologise for the hastiness of my assistant, Miss Hampton.' A pause. 'Please, let us begin again. Can I fix you a drink? ...'

I turned my back on the conversation playing out on the screen. I was a little too fazed already to start repeating myself over in my head. I never enjoyed watching myself on screen, particularly when I'd been recorded unconsciously. I made my way through to the other room where Lotte was still sitting, crouched over her tiny computer pad.

'Hey you.'

She looked up, pushing her hair back behind her ear once again.

'Hi. How's it going?'

'Pretty badly, I think. Someone managed to scramble Spinoza so there's no recording of the crime. And I'm feeling pretty wrecked. When we get out of here, can we just head back to your place to crash out?'

'Of course. I guessed you'd be staying over for a few days. We can take it easy. Try and forget about what's happened.' She smiled. 'I know it's not going to be that easy. But we can try.'

I reached out and took the mug of cold coffee from her hand. I took a long swig, and then gave it back. 'No, it's not going to be easy at all. But thanks for being there.' I bent over and kissed her brightly on the forehead. 'Perhaps tomorrow we can ... Hang on.'

Lotte looked up at me, perplexed. I pushed my way back

through to the other room. I'd just overheard a part of the conversation that I didn't recall from the other day. I tried to get the attention of the AI who was controlling the playback. 'Excuse me, can we just see that bit again. About thirty seconds ago. She said something that I didn't remember.'

The AI rolled the images backward on the screen for a few moments, and then cut them free to play out again. I watched intently from behind one of the other human officers.

'... Yes, I was most saddened at the news of your uncle's death ...'

'Indeed, but I admit to being not too surprised. Latterly he'd been spending far too much time with his head in his books and not enough time worrying about his estate. There isn't a week goes by when a family such as mine doesn't receive threatening messages or blackmail attempts from various pressure groups, and Uncle Julian had taken to ignoring them, at his own peril.' A slight pause. 'He'd hardly been near the old house for months, preferring to spend his time away on long field trips into the interior, indulging his silly obsession with ancient history. The Policzia even suggested that there was evidence of a trespasser when they searched the house, but couldn't find anything missing. He'd been off in the interior for nearly a month when he died, out on the fells in a collapsible coral dome. His assistant found him there one morning, hunched over his desk. The commissioning AI reported a final verdict of death by natural causes. It's all a very sorry state of affairs. Of course ...' another pregnant pause, '... you realise that this is to go no further? ...'

Officer Tribauer turned to me and shrugged. 'These rich families are always getting themselves into trouble. Though she's right, you know – there isn't a week goes by without a threatening message of some sort. Never come to anything though. He probably got bitten by a spider or snake or something, out there on the hills.' He turned back to the screen.

I glanced down at the floor, at Pharo's body. Tiny silver spiders were still running all over him, covering his face and swarming into his nostrils and ears. I grimaced, and took a step backwards towards the other room. 'Am I free to go? I think I could do with some fresh air. I'm starting to feel a little faint.'

The AI in the corner looked up, and traced the red glow of its sensor array over my face.

'Of course. We can offer you an escort back to Miss Robeaux's apartment if you wish?'

I glanced back at Lotte, who was watching me attentively. 'That really won't be necessary,' I said. 'I can take my own transport. One thing, though – I could do with a couple of my books?'

Officer Tribauer put his hand on my shoulder. 'I'm afraid we're going to have to hang on to those, Mr Mihajlovic. Evidence, you see.'

I shrugged noncommittally. 'If that's the way we have to do it ...'

'No, it will be all right,' a metallic voice cut in from the other side of the room. 'Feel free to take as many of your books as you wish, Mr Mihajlovic. I'm sure we won't be needing them. We will be sure to inform you as soon as we are done here.'

I made my way to the back of the room and gingerly used my palmprint to open the lock on the book cabinet. The front panel slid open with a metallic hiss. I reached inside and removed the two volumes of the Roch, as well as the Roberts book on historical architecture.

When I turned back, Lotte was waiting for me by the door.

'Come on, let's get you home.' She slipped a reassuring arm around my shoulders. ' I can't see why you need those bloody books though?'

I left the answer hanging on the tip of my tongue.

I made my way out towards the shop front, glancing back into the office for one last look at the remains of my friend, violated and bloody on the floor. My eyes met with the blank, skeletal face of the AI in the corner of the room, and I noticed, unnervingly, that it was watching me intently as I left. I shivered as I stepped out into the morning sunlight and reached into my pocket for a smoke.

Too late, I realised that I had left my packet of cigarettes inside.

Six

'The first hole made through a piece of stone is a revelation.'
Henry Moore, from The Listener *(1937, Earth Standard)*

What is the nature of epiphany? Must it always strike as lightning, a sparking, dramatic revelation cast directly into the mind of some unwary recipient? Or can it creep insidiously into one's consciousness, beginning with the slightest of doubts and then later, after being exercised and provoked by a myriad of forces, grow into something more substantial, more worthy of note? I believe that it develops, piecemeal, as facts are collated and notions put to the test.

And in my case, I was sure, the revelation was only just around the corner. It started with a dream.

They were sawing off my left hand as I lay curled up on the floor in a tight ball, attempting to stave off the kicks that were thundering into my head and back with piston-like fury. Pain blossomed into white light as the teeth of the molecular saw bit into my flesh and bone, carving my arm into great ribbons of blood and gore. The pounding of their boots against my head continued unabated.

Eventually, after what seemed like hours of constant abuse, I felt my skull give way. Warm blood slipped out across the tiles, drenching the back of my neck and running in dark rivulets over my shoulders and down my back. The remaining part of my forearm was twitching furiously as my lifeblood pumped out into the cold, empty room. My left hand was a ghost, and I clenched the fingers into an angry fist as if they were still there. I could hear nothing but the heady rush of my own blood, vacating my body with ready abandon. My breath gurgled rudely in my fluid-filled lungs. And then I noticed the mechanical spiders that had begun to crawl all over me, their tiny legs prickling my skin like a thousand miniature needles. They swarmed towards every orifice, forcing themselves into my mouth and pushing their way through the very pores of my skin, slipping easily into my bloodstream. I knew then, at that point, which hung like a moment suspended in time, that in a matter of seconds I was going to cease to exist. The microscopic machines swimming through my bloodstream were about to rewrite my very mind and turn my neural pathways into a messy soup of atoms.

I woke in a cold sweat. Lotte was crouched over me, dabbing at my forehead with a cool cloth. I sat forward, checking that my left hand was still in place, attached at the wrist. I flexed my fingers just to be sure, cradling Lotte's hand in my own. The back of my neck was damp with perspiration. I gestured for Lotte to give me the flannel, and placed it against the nape of my neck to cool me down. Lotte reached over and cupped my face in her hands, kissing me softly on the cheek. Her lips left a cool, damp impression on my skin.

'Were you dreaming about Jonah?' Her face was a picture of concern.

I nodded to indicate that I didn't want to discuss the matter.

'There's nothing you can do now, Rehan. It's in the hands of the Policzia.'

'That's what I'm worried about.'

'Look, let me fix you something to eat, and we can talk it over.' She disappeared into the kitchen with a quick hop, which was shortly followed by the sound of rattling pans. 'What do you fancy? I've got some spiced Calk cheese if you fancy an omelette?'

'Whatever.'

I cast my eyes around the room. I felt like shit. Whatever it was that the AI had injected me with was still working its way through my veins. I felt hollow, drained of all energy. My mind was spinning into overdrive. I didn't even feel like I could smoke a cigarette. I pushed myself up to my feet and made my way unsteadily over to the wall-mounted netscreen. Lotte was still in the kitchen, noisily preparing some food. I put a hand on the wall and leaned in towards the screen. The AI intuited my intention and the small area of plastiform before my face mirrored over with a soft gleam. Light refracted off its surface like little lemon stars. I looked myself over. My face was gaunt and bloodless, and my skin looked waxy, like that of a corpse. Dark circles formed bruised, ring-shaped recesses around my eyes, and my eyes themselves had taken on a sickly yellow hue instead of their usual milky-white shine. Powdery black particles dusted my upper lip, underneath my nostrils. I brushed them away with my finger. Nanotech ash. Some virus was taking my internal systems apart, piece by piece.

I staggered backwards towards the sofa, but missed my footing and stumbled over onto the floor, jarring my elbow badly on the coffee table. I allowed myself to sink back onto the soft carpet, my body smarting from the fall. The room was spinning around me, and I was worried that I was going to lose consciousness any minute. I saw Lotte put her head around the doorframe to see what the commotion was. When she saw me lying on the floor, she dashed in to check that I was all right.

'Oh Rehan, what are you doing to yourself?' She leaned over me and put her hand on my forehead, her face a picture of concern. 'God, you're burning up. Let me get you some ice or something ...' As she made to leave, I reached up and grabbed her arm, staying her.

'No, Lotte, listen to me. You need to get me to a nanotech clinic. I think I've got a virus that's attacking my internal systems.' I stopped to splutter a rattling cough. 'Nowhere anyone will know me, though. Don't tell anyone where we're going. If I pass out, just make sure you get me there. The technicians can do the rest.' I blinked rapidly to try to keep myself from slipping away.

'Christ, okay. Where do you want me to go? Oh God, I haven't got any idea!' She stood up, looking frantic. 'Shit, the food's burning in there.' She ran into the kitchen and I heard her fling the pans into the sink. Moments later she was back in the living room, collecting her things. 'I'll take you to see Jacq. Jacq will sort you out.' She was mumbling to herself incoherently. I could feel myself drifting away, stage by stage. Everything had taken on a dream-like quality.

'I don't know, Lotte. Just do whatever you can. The key-print to my aerofoil is in my jacket pocket.' My voice was a rasp, raw and painful.

Lotte rummaged around in my jacket until she found the key.

'Okay, can you walk?'

'I don't think so. Maybe if you support me I can make it to the aerofoil.'

She stepped over me and hauled me up by my armpits. I slouched forward, trying to help her get me onto my feet. She knelt down beside me and I slung my arm up over her shoulders. We struggled together to get me standing up and walking.

The last thing I remember before darkness hit me like a wave of thick, black ink was the kiss of fresh air against my face as we made our way out through the door and into the blinding sunshine outside.

Much of what followed occurred to me as a series of impressions, or dreams. The journey to see Jacq is a complex and messy web of images that remains completely impenetrable in the archive of my brain. I had little or no machine assistance to stop me from slipping into and out of consciousness, and dreams began to pepper reality to the extent that I am now, looking back, unable satisfactorily to separate the two.

I remember coming to in a dark, humid waiting room, laid out on a hard wooden bench whilst Lotte sat conversing with a young woman across the other side of the room. The girl wore a smart, severely cut shirt that made her pert breasts poke out like tectonic ruptures and a short skirt that was hitched up to show off her tanned, shapely legs. She toyed constantly with her hands, fidgeting anxiously as if she were waiting for something, or someone else, to arrive. She smiled at me sweetly when she noticed I was awake, and then turned her attention back to Lotte, who was conversing with her in low, whispering tones. Presently, the blackness swam out of the light to reclaim me.

The next time I woke was with a sharp start. My eyes took a few moments to focus. I was propped up in a comfortable folding chair, my arms and legs clipped into restraints by my side. A man was leaning over me, examining my eyes with a large looking glass. He stepped back and quickly folded into focus. He was fat, and dressed in a dirty leather smock that was streaked with black soot and all manner of grease and grime. Underneath this he wore a one-piece coverall that looked like it had seen better days. He stroked his bald head as if he longed nostalgically for a lock of his long-lost golden hair. He fixed his eyes on me and chuckled to himself, sinisterly.

'Ah, Miss Robeaux, our beautiful sleeper is awake.' I noticed he held a spent hypo-tube in his left hand. Lotte appeared beside me. I craned my neck to try to look at her.

'No, Rehan, don't try to move. Jacq has just given you a quick shot to wake you up a bit. He's going to give you a full tech-flush to get this virus out of your system. Then he can flood you out again with a new set of nanotech. You sit back and try not to worry, everything is going to be OK.' She smiled stoically, as if she didn't really believe what she was telling me. I tried to nod to her in reassurance, although I felt little enough of that myself. A moment later, she disappeared from view. Jacq reappeared, carting a large hypo-gun and a trigger-happy look on his face. He smiled warmly.

'I'm afraid this is going to hurt quite a bit.' By the look on his face, he was enjoying every moment of it. He reached into his pocket and pulled out a small metal bar, which he pushed into my mouth. It tasted bitter and dirty, like it had been used a few hundred times before and had never been sterilised.

'Here, bite on that. It may help a little.'

He adjusted his posture until he was straddling the chair, his face inordinately close to my own. His breath was stale and foul, like rotten food. His eyes gleamed as he clasped my head in his left hand and held me still.

Then, with one sudden movement, he jabbed the hypo-gun viscously underneath my chin and fired it into the soft flesh at the top of my throat. He sprang backwards, clattering into a small trestle table and sending a tray of his equipment crashing to the floor.

'There. Now we wait.' He disappeared again from view.

There was a rush of blood to my head. For a moment, it was as if I was floating on pure oxygen. Everything cleared and my sensorium felt crisp and sharp, as if all the neural pathways in my brain had suddenly been revitalised and refreshed. My whole body felt alert. Then I exploded in pain.

Every single pore erupted as the dying nanomachines were ejected from my body. I clenched down on the bit, stifling a scream as one of my teeth shattered on the hard metal and the shrapnel shred the inside of my mouth. It felt like I was on fire. I was bleeding from every pore, every orifice. The remains of the nanos were rupturing out of my body, tearing through muscle and flesh, pushing their way out of my tear ducts and from underneath my fingernails. My eyes flooded with blood, and I tried to blink it away, succeeding only in making things worse. My entire body was racked in agony. I wondered if dying would have been less painful.

Eventually, the pain subsided and I was left sagging in the chair, delirious. The bit had fallen out of my mouth at some point during the tech-flush and I had bitten through my lower lip. Jacq dabbed at it with an antiseptic swab. My clothes were soaked through with blood. It was in my hair, in my eyes, up my nose. My breath wheezed in and out of my lungs with an agonised moan, whistling with every forced exhalation. The two of them released me from the arm and leg restraints, and I fell forward into Lotte's arms. I heard Jacq's low, rumbling voice somewhere in the background, like an earthquake, trembling through my bones.

'Right. First we get him cleaned up. Then we fill him up again.'

I was dragged through to another room, where I was stripped by the young girl from reception and pushed underneath a hot, steaming shower. I closed my eyes and let the water play over me as I slumped against the tiled wall. The blood rinsed off me in a red deluge. After a while, the water stopped, and I sat there shivering in the cold draught, trying to cover my nakedness. I felt small and pathetic, sitting there naked in the back room of some seedy barbershop, completely out of control. I think I may have even fallen asleep again, exhausted.

I was brought round by a blast of warm air that came up from the floor, in which I rubbed myself down cautiously, trying to dry off after the shower. My skin was aflame with a thousand puncture wounds. Even my penis was distended and sore. I passed water in a dirty urinal in the corner of the room. The young woman from reception returned after I had finished and laid out a clean coverall and underwear on the back of a chair. I tore open the sterile, plastic packet and took the coverall out, dressing as quickly as I could. Lotte was waiting for me in the other room.

'Christ, was that really necessary?' I looked past Lotte to the bulky form of Jacq, who was hunched over his trestle table rearranging his instruments of torture. Lotte looked pained.

'Jacq's taken a look at a sample of your blood whilst you were cleaning yourself up.'

'And ...'

'And it wasn't a virus. Your nanotech was being sabotaged. Something had caused the nanos to mutate, and they were actually attacking you from the inside. We need to get you filled up again as quickly as possible – the new machines may have some repair work to do on your internal organs.'

I pushed my way past Lotte to stand next to Jacq. He placed another hypo-gun carefully down on a steel tray with a loud, metallic click. I could feel a sharp pain rising steadily in my lower abdomen. I tried to put it out of mind.

'What could have caused this sort of mutation? I've never heard of it before. Have you?'

He turned to me, almost nonchalantly. 'It's a classic assassination technique.' He rubbed his hands on his dirty smock. 'Very effective, leaves no trace and the subject is usually well away from the scene before they begin to notice the effects. A crime like this is incredibly hard to pin on anyone.' He smiled. 'Think of anyone who's out to kill you, Mr Mihajlovic?'

I shuddered, and turned towards Lotte, who had suddenly turned as white as a sheet.

I couldn't help thinking of old Julian Hampton, slumped over his desk with his pen still clutched tightly in his hand, and Jonah Pharo, splayed out in a bloody mess on the cold tiles of my office floor. Someone was very intent on keeping the contents of those books a secret.

I turned back to Jacq just in time to see the second hypo-gun descending on me from behind.

Seven

'Pale Death with impartial tread beats at the poor man's cottage door and at the palaces of kings.'
Horace, Odes *(65BC-8BC Earth Standard)*

I sometimes question if we are right to strive for immortality. Can the human mind subsist on life alone, or does it temper with age, become a bloated, swollen thing that struggles to search out new experience or seek out satisfaction? Do the minds of machines suffer from the same condition? Perhaps we die to stop our lives becoming tepid, to halt the steady digression into self-obsession and egotism. Reboot technology gave Lotte a reason to live – although that soon developed into introspection and an attraction to self-abuse – but in some ways it almost seemed as if it was Lotte, or people like her, who gave rebooting a reason to exist. And the question remained – was her machine intellect a true representation of the person she had been, given that she now had no recollection of her own traumatic demise?

I wondered these things as I stepped out of the barbershop feeling like a new man.

The new nanotech coursed through my body like live electricity.

I could feel the microscopic machines repairing my tired body, rewriting my very genes from the inside out, affecting new modifications and revitalising my internal systems. I breathed deeply and tasted the fresh tang of the air, as my lungs began to flush my body with oxygen. I was keenly aware of everything that was happening around me, heightened by the changes the machines were making to my senses. Jacq had shot me up with a high-grade, military breed of machine that – he told me afterwards – he had sampled from a decomposing corpse and cloned in a thick vat of neurofluid in the back room of his shop. As much as the notion disgusted me, I had to admit that I felt better than I had in some time. The nanotech sharpened my senses and quickened my pulse. The residual pain of the tech-flush was already subsiding and I felt fresh, ready and alert. My skin, after years of growing soft and fat, was once again tight and wiry on my frame. I wondered, briefly, if this was what it felt like to be rebooted.

Lotte, it transpired, knew Jacq from the early years of her reboot, when he had cut her a number of genetic alterations, reshaping her newly cloned body in an effort to help heal her, to distance her new self from that of her previous incarnation. Apparently it was common amongst reboots; they needed to feel that they were more than just a shadow of their old lives, to define for themselves a wedge of individuality. Lotte and Jacq were intimately familiar – their body language suggested that there was much more than just a passing acquaintance between them, more than the typical relationship between a patient and her surgeon. I let it pass, riding it out. Jacq had done me a real favour, and whatever had passed between the two of them had been, I was sure, a moment of nostalgia rather than a rekindling of passion. At least that's what I told myself, as we rounded a bend and made our way out onto the bustle and flow of the freeway.

I sat at the wheel of the aerofoil as we made our way back towards Lotte's place. We needed to get away, to lie low for a few days, but first I wanted to collect a few things and make a couple of calls. Anna Hampton wasn't telling me the whole story and I needed to find out what she knew. With Pharo already dead, and at least one attempt on my own life, I was thinking about cutting myself out of the deal and handing the books back to Hampton for her to dispose of by herself. Only, I knew I was already too deeply involved and the mystery would keep eating away at me, cancer-like, until I managed to bring it to some satisfactory conclusion. Parts of the puzzle were already starting to click into place, but I was missing something fundamental, some final clue that would illuminate everything and bring it all to a head. It was like having all the pieces of a jigsaw laid out on a table and not knowing what picture they were supposed to make. And after my experience at Jacq's, I was growing more and more suspicious of the Policzia.

It all hinged on the column in the Roberts book and on what Julian Hampton had found, out there in the hills.

Lotte was having a hard time understanding what was going on. She kept looking at me from across the cabin of the vehicle, or placing a gentle hand on my knee, murmuring softly underneath her breath.

'Oh, Rehan. Oh, Rehan.'

I didn't know what to tell her. I didn't even know what to tell myself. I tried to reassure her, to impress upon her that everything was going to be okay, but I knew I was having trouble sounding convincing. Someone was out to kill me, and I had the horrible notion that they wouldn't hesitate to take out Lotte too.

I reached out and placed my hand, briefly, gently, on Lotte's arm. Moments later I pulled away, shuddering, as I was shaken by a vision of thousands of tiny silver spiders, swarming like a heaving blanket over Pharo's mutilated corpse. I tried to put it out of mind.

From the outside, Lotte's apartment looked deserted. I pulled the aerofoil to a stop a little way up the street, scanning around, trying to pick up on any parked vehicles or incongruous pedestrians that could be keeping an eye on the place. I was inexperienced in this sort of roadside surveillance, but to my untrained eye, everything appeared to be clear. I released the door catch on the aerofoil and clambered out into the street. Lotte followed close behind me.

Moments later, I was patching a call through the netscreen to Anna Hampton. Behind me, in the other room, Lotte was beginning to throw some of her clothes into a holdall. The apartment still smelled of stale, burnt food. I lit myself a cigarette and watched for a few seconds as the netscreen buzzed with a pool of chaotic static, before Anna Hampton's face slowly coalesced on the surface as if she was pushing her way up through a layer of murky water, gently breaking surface tension. She looked tired and dishevelled, and not too pleased at being disturbed. A virtual backdrop, showing a brightly lit glade filled with twittering birds and leafy trees, dropped in seamlessly behind her.

'Mr Mihajlovic, I can give you five minutes. Do you have some good news for me?' Her stern expression stared out from the screen, her impatience evident by the set of her lips. I let her wait for a moment before answering.

'Quite the opposite, I'm afraid.' I let that hang. 'There's been an attempted robbery at my office and my assistant has been found dead. They cut his hand off so they could try and get past the security system and steal your books.' I tried to keep my voice even and calm. Anna Hampton drew in a sharp breath and all the blood drained out of her face.

'I presume the books are still in your possession, Mr Mihajlovic. I would hate to …'

I cut her off. 'The books are fine, for fuck's sake, which is more than I can say for my friend. And what's more, I've just had to suffer the humiliation and pain of a tech-flush, as it now seems that someone is thinking about taking me out of the equation too. I'm seriously considering bringing our agreement to an end …'

'Now, don't you think you may be overreacting a little? If it's a case of money, we can talk figures … I know I may have been a little harsh on you when we first discussed terms.'

'Jesus Christ, I'm not talking about money here! I'm talking about not being insured for a fucking reboot if one of those crazy bastards catches up with me! What is it about these books that would have people so fired up?' I fixed her angrily in my gaze from across the room.

'Well, they are worth a great deal of money ...' She was stalling, and she knew it.

'I think we both know there's a little more to it than that. What did your uncle find out on his expeditions into the interior? Is that why they finished him off, too?'

'Come now, Mr Mihajlovic, I think you're letting your imagination run away with you a little. Uncle Julian was just an old quack. He'd got it into his head that he was on the verge of making a great archaeological discovery out in the hills. He poured all the family money into his stupid little dream and never turned up a jot. I think it was the realisation that he was never going to find anything that eventually killed him. If you're really that bothered, I can show you his notes.'

'He made notes? And you have them?'

'There's a box of his old junk knocking around the house somewhere. Look, I really have to get going.' She glanced back at something, or someone, off screen, 'Drop round later and we can talk it over. If you like, we can talk to my AI about getting you some insurance while we're at it. I'm truly sorry about your friend, but I do need you to sell those books. Without the extra cash, there's no way I'm going to be able to hold on to the estate.'

'I ...' I started, but she had already retreated out of view. 'I don't give a damn about you keeping your estate ...' I finished. I was sure that she hadn't heard me. I sat back, and stared at the screen, thinking. At least if I went over to the Hampton place I'd have a chance to take a look at the column in the garden. There had to be a link there between that and the picture of the column in the book. We could swing by there on our way to the Scattership port. I glanced back at the screen. The idyllic view of the wooded glade shimmered silently out of view, to be replaced by the usual puddle of dirty static. I pushed myself up to my feet and went to find Lotte in the bedroom. She was sitting on the edge of the bed, surrounded by piles of clothes that she had pulled out of the wardrobe and flung across the room. The holdall was lying empty by her feet. Her face was buried in her hands and her shoulders heaved as she finally allowed herself to break down in tears. I sat down next to her and wrapped my arms around her shoulders. She fell against me, and continued to sob.

'Everything is going to be okay. Everything is going to be okay.' I repeated the mantra softly under my breath, kissing her vanilla hair and holding her tightly in my arms. After a few moments, she looked up at me, imploringly.

'Look. I'm not going to come with you. I could stay here while you go away for a few days. Someone needs to take care of arrangements for Jonah. I'll still be here when you get back. You don't need to take me away to the jungle with you.'

I could feel my heart breaking as it dawned on me just how much I was putting her through, how fragile her carefully constructed reality really was. I hushed her gently and rocked her backwards and forwards like a small child. 'It's not safe here at the moment. I can't guarantee that you'd be okay. I need to keep you with me for a while. Just bear with me, Lotte, and everything will work itself out.'

'What the hell have you got yourself involved in, Rehan, that people are trying to kill you?'

'I don't know. I really don't. But I'm going to have to try to find out. Now, let's get this packing finished and we can be on our way.' I reached down, picked up the holdall and starting stuffing in handfuls of the clothes that had spilt upon the floor like a landslide of silk and chenille.

An hour later, we pulled up at the front of the Hampton building, our bags and the handful of books that I'd brought with me scattered about untidily on the back seat. At the other end of the driveway, a man was climbing back into the driving seat of a blue aerofoil. I allowed my eyes to zoom in a little closer, closing the distance between us. I couldn't quite make out the man's face, but he was wearing a dark, heavy beard and his hair was closely cropped, or shaven. He looked large, muscular, and too big for the controls. Another, more indistinct figure was crouched beside him in the passenger seat. I blinked my eyes back to normality. I didn't think they'd seen us. I reversed the aerofoil quietly behind a row of large bushes, and waited. Lotte started to say something, but I put my finger to my lips and gestured for her to lie low. Moments later, the couple sped past in their blue vehicle, leaving a trail of dust billowing up into the air like the exhalation of a cigarette, or the tail end of a storm.

I pulled the aerofoil back out onto the driveway and parked it up under the shade of a large oak tree. I collected the books from the back seat and dumped them into a knapsack I'd brought along for the purpose. I wasn't going to take any more chances by leaving them unattended in the back of the aerofoil. Lotte climbed out of the passenger seat behind me.

'My God, look at this place ...' She stood with her hands in her trouser pockets, staring up at the great house. 'It's like something I'd imagine from Old Earth.' Her eyes were shining with wonder and surprise. I pointed to the walls.

'Can you see where the programmed coral runs around the doorway? And the way the house just seems to rise out of the ground like a mountain or something?'

'It's magnificent.'

'Just wait 'til you see the staircase. C'mon.'

We began making our way along the narrow pathway that led up to the house. Presently, the tall, dominating silhouette of Trajan's Column loomed into view. Lotte was quick to point it out to me.

'Look at that! What do you think it is?' It was as if the wonder of seeing the fairytale house and garden had suddenly banished all the fright and anxiety of the previous couple of days. I hoped I was going to be able to keep it that way.

'It's a replica of Trajan's Column, an ancient monument from Earth. Let's go and take a closer look.'

I stepped off the path and made long strides across the carefully-manicured lawn. It smelled fresh, dewy, as if it had just been cut. It had obviously been heavily genengineered, like most of the surrounding landscape. It probably hadn't been physically cut for centuries. I looked back to make sure that Lotte was following behind me. She hesitated for a moment, then skipped quickly across the grass, trying to keep up.

The column was situated to the left of the great house, tall and prominent against the surrounding trees. Around it, the grass and bushes had been allowed to grow wild, running riot in a cacophony of greens and browns. I pushed my way through, the wet leaves leaving damp stains on my trousers, little shiny beads on my boots.

The column stood proudly on top of a large, stone plinth, its white marble elegance glistening in the waning light. It was covered in images: intricate, worn pictograms that circled around it, rising in a continuous sequence right up to its pinnacle. I allowed my fingers to trail gently over them whilst I tried to work out what they meant. The figures were tired and worn, but I could just about make out what was happening. A procession of warriors rode into battle on the backs of their steeds. Behind them, they dragged ancient, deadly war machines and fended off attacks from a number of different flanks. I moved around the column, following the chain of events. It seemed to tell a story. Trajan, who I presumed was the warrior who led the assault, rode into battle with an army of his soldiers. Here pictograms showed him decimating his enemies with the edge of his sword, there he fended off returning blows with his great shield. Eventually, he rode back to his homeland a battle-scarred champion. It was a tribute to victory, a story set in stone. I couldn't even begin to imagine how many thousands of years ago the events in the story had taken place, on a distant planet on the other side of the galaxy. I felt awed at the magnificence of it all. Yet it nevertheless struck me, why would anyone conceive to create a replica of such a monument, here in the garden of an old house, thousands of light years away from where it was ever relevant? It had to have something to do with the other column in the Roberts book, the column to which Julian Hampton had made reference in his notes. I had the feeling that there was some ironic comment being made, some other, deeper meaning that would become clear only when I finally managed to take a look at the monument in the hills. I was convinced that this replica was not just a folly created by the mad old eccentric that Anna Hampton believed her uncle to be. And what's more, it suggested that there had to be another story of some sort, wrapped around that other tower of stone, somewhere deep in the interior. I had no idea what it could be, but I resolved to find out as soon as I could.

I looked around. Lotte had wandered off into the garden, tiptoeing carefully between the flowerbeds. I called over to her.

'Shall we head into the house?'

'Whatever.' She was lost in the grandeur of the garden, like a child impressed by the carefully shaped topiary of a maze. I caught up with her and took her gently by the arm.

'C'mon. We've got a flight to catch after we're done here.'

We made our way up to the gaping darkness of the main entrance.

I stepped inside, ducking my head a little to avoid knocking it on the low beam. In the hallway, everything was still. I knew immediately that something was wrong; the hairs stood up on the back of my neck and I had to fight off a shiver. Behind me, Lotte was taking in the dilapidated staircase and the ancient trees that wound their boughs around it like a protective mother.

The air was shot through with an empty silence. I raised my voice, with trepidation. 'Miss Hampton? Are you home? It's Rehan Mihajlovic here ...' My voice echoed away into the dusty corners of the hallway.

Nothing.

I made my way to the reception room where I'd spoken to Anna Hampton the previous day. The door was slightly ajar. I pushed it open with my hand, and gingerly stepped inside. 'Hello ...?'

She was sitting in a chair by the fireplace, her legs curled up underneath her and her head lolling easily to one side, quietly asleep. Behind her, static danced on the netscreen with a low hiss. I moved towards her, expecting her to wake up. 'Miss Hampton? Hello?' There was no response. I felt rude and embarrassed for intruding on her personal space.

I cleared my throat and put my hand out to shake her gently by the arm. My fingers brushed against her hand. Her flesh was icy. I pulled back, shocked. She looked like she wasn't breathing. 'Anna? Anna, wake up.' I put my fingers against the soft skin of her throat, searching for a pulse. Her head flopped to one side at my touch, her mouth falling open with a sudden, deathly slackness.

I watched in horror as hundreds of tiny metallic spiders began to spill out from underneath her tongue, scattering across her chin and falling like silver raindrops onto the still mountains of her breasts. I stumbled backwards, calling out to Lotte in the hallway.

'Lotte? Are you there, Lotte?'

'My God, Rehan, what's wrong?'

'Lotte. Run. Run now, as fast as you can.'

Eight

'Violence is the key to all evolutionary systems, human or otherwise.'
J. Rupert Walters, Evolutionary Systems and the Bioelectric Cloning Process *(189 Copernica Standard)*

We shot out of the driveway in the aerofoil, slamming the brakes on hard to take the corner at high speed. The gravitational compensators worked to steady the vehicle and prevent our bodies from slamming sideways against the doors, but I still managed to crack my hand painfully against the dashboard. Moments later the nanotech cut in and deadened the pain. Jacq had given me some good shit.

I grabbed at the steering clasp and directed us straight for the nearest freeway, trying to hold it steady whilst we were buffeted in different directions by the force of the oncoming traffic. We passed down a slip road and out onto the main tributary, which in turn fed into the busy midsection of the freeway. A soft chime sounded from somewhere behind me, and a blinking icon appeared on the dashboard by the edge of the steering clasp. I pawed at it readily, happily relinquishing control of the vehicle to the freeway guidance system that monitored all the traffic passing into and out of the city. The steering clasp began to shift underneath my fingers, moving of its own volition. We slowed considerably, then slipped out into the middle of a steady stream of traffic. I sat back and tried to relax.

'What the fuck is going on?'

I turned and blinked at Lotte, bewildered.

'What do you mean?'

'I mean – "Run as fast as you fucking can!" I mean nearly killing us by accelerating around a corner with your foot to the floor. Are you going to tell me what the hell is going on, or do I have to wait for my supernatural sixth sense to kick in and explain it all?' She glowered at me, more evidently scared than angry.

I stammered for a minute, undecided how much to tell her, then fixed her with an even glare. 'She was dead. I went into the room and she was dead. Propped up in a chair with her head flopped on one side. And the little machines were everywhere.' I hesitated for a moment, cleared my throat. 'They were all over the place, in her mouth, in her hair. Those tiny spiders they dusted the shop with when Pharo ...' I indicated with my fingers. There was a lump in my throat. 'They're trying to take us out, one by one.'

There was a stunned silence from the other side of the cabin.

'Who? Who are trying to take you out?'

'I don't know!' I felt exasperated, like wringing my hands or tearing my hair out. 'But I do know it's got something to do with those books we've got stashed on the back seat.'

'Let's get rid of them, then ...' She tried to reach around, fumbling amongst the bags piled up on the back seat, searching out my knapsack.

'It won't do any good. It's too late for that. I've already asked the wrong questions. Look at poor Anna Hampton. She didn't even know what was in the books. To her, they were just a bit of extra cash, an old family heirloom that she needed to get rid of. And look what happened to her.'

'We'll take it to the Policzia then.'

'Lotte.' I half turned towards her in the seat, taking her hands in my own, imploring her to understand. 'They're in on it. Why else do you think we had to get over to Jacq's place and flush all that dirty nanotech out of my system? It was the injection the AI gave me after my interview. And those spiders. All over the Hampton place and not a sign of any officers or patrol vehicles for miles. It was Officer Tribauer that gave it away, back when he was talking about Julian Hampton and his expeditions into the interior. "Probably got bitten by a spider or something up in the hills," he said.' I shivered, suddenly cold. 'But he didn't say whether the spider was biological or not. What you've got to understand is that something happened, something right back in the early days of the colony, and someone is trying very hard to make sure that no-one else finds out about it.'

Lotte was staring at me, wide-eyed with panic. 'Oh my God. Rehan, what are we going to do?'

'We're going to stick to the plan. We're getting out of here as soon as we can. We'll head into the interior for a few days, take a little place in some village or town. We'll lie low and let it all blow over. *Trust me* – everything is going to be okay.' I wish I'd felt so sure of that myself. She sat back in her seat, unsure what to say or how to react.

Up ahead, the exit for the Scattership port was flagging up on the windscreen as a huge, holographic icon. I tapped at the dashboard and the aerofoil chimed to let me know that it was once again under my control. I swung it round deftly into the correct lane and the icon pixelated and bled away. Lotte was very still in the seat beside me, staring out of the windscreen at the oscillating horizon.

Scatterships filled the air in the distance, jetting up into the sky on great plumes of light to scrape at the atmosphere, leaving long, grey trails of smoke and fusion in their wake. Directly ahead, above the acres of land that comprised the port itself, a number of them were dropping sharply out of the sky, preparing to set down on the immense runways like so many airborne ducks coming in to land.

I glanced at the top left-hand corner of the windscreen and a box opened up, feeding me the view from the rear sensor array. A blue aerofoil, similar to my own, was squatting on the road behind us, three or four places back in the queue. My heart stepped up a gear. I zoomed in on the image and tried to catch sight of the driver. I couldn't quite make him out; the lights from the Scatterships overhead were refracting on the surface of his windscreen, partially obscuring him from view. I saw him shift anxiously in his seat, as if impatient to get to his destination. I moved out into the nearside lane and started to gather some speed. Glancing back, I saw the blue aerofoil disappearing into the mesh of traffic behind us. I leaned back into my seat and the image faded slowly from the corner of the screen.

'The sooner we get out of here, the better,' I said to no one in particular.

Lotte didn't even seem to acknowledge that I'd spoken. Everything was quiet except the gentle purr of the engines and the hum of distant orbital traffic coming in to land.

The approach to the Scattership port was a long, narrow road flanked by a motley assortment of shops, cafes and hyperterminals. Side streets veered off at sharp right-angles at various points along its length. I pulled the aerofoil to a stop outside one of the nearby hyperterminals and clambered out onto the busy thoroughfare. Lotte waited inside, her head resting up against the window as if she was trying to sleep. I wondered what was going through her mind. She hadn't spoken since our earlier exchange, and the thick, syrupy tension it was generating between us was starting to get to me. I needed to find a way through it, to make her understand how important it was that we found out exactly what was going on, but I was having trouble getting a hold on the guilt of being responsible for putting her in danger in the first place. Not to mention the weight of Pharo's death, bearing down on me like an oppressive, snarling animal. I had to focus.

I looked around. The sky was the colour of raw amber, burnt by the constant emissions of the Scattership engines and the plumes of fusion power that lifted them up into orbit. On an impulse, I reached into the back of the aerofoil and snatched up the knapsack containing the three books. Around me, people were scurrying about their business like ants, worrying their way into buildings or shops, pushing each other out of the way to make room. I ducked into the doorway of the hyperterminal, narrowly avoiding being jostled out of the way by an angry mother dragging her two children down the street by their arms.

'Oh, come *on!*'

The hyperterminal was a small room decked out with sixteen or seventeen base level AIs and a couple of private booths at the back for the more discerning or 'specialist' clientele. It wouldn't have surprised me to find out that they contained full holofield generators or virtugraphic interfaces. The place was lit with a soft purple glow, and muzak tinkled quietly in the background, just audible enough for it not to be too obtrusive. I tried to catch the attention of one of the human staff, who trundled his way over when he noticed me looking around like I needed some help. He was dressed in a baggy blue uniform emblazoned with the sickle-shaped logo of his employers, and his hair was tied back in a long, brown ponytail. He stood with his hands jabbed deep inside his pockets, staring down at the floor. I looked again at the logo on his top pocket. The intuitive code underpinning it must have noticed that it had my attention and shot out a spray of light, circling through a gaudy array of images and icons. I watched the holographic presentation cycle through twice before I made eye contact with the man himself.

Welcome to Solaria 7. Offering a full range of intuitive holofield suites and Class 19 base terminals for your every need. My name is Steve. How can I be of assistance?

He shrugged. 'Can I help you?'

'Yeah, I just need five minutes on one of your base terminals. Nothing special. I only want to make a couple of calls.'

He turned slightly to indicate a line of empty terminals blinking out into the room behind him. 'Take your pick. Just slot your credit chip into the interface and go for your life. Max time is thirty minutes.'

'I only need five,' I repeated, and he sloped off again to see to the private booths at the back of the room. I picked a nearby terminal and jacked my credit chip in, kneeling down onto one of the plush cushions that covered the floor and bringing my face level with the screen. The avatar of the onboard AI stared back at me like a skeletal apparition in a mirror.

'Get me a ticket agency,' I said, squaring up to the AI, slightly uncomfortable. 'I need two tickets for a sub-orbital flight. One way.' It disappeared suddenly from view, without even a flicker of emotion to mar the porcelain elegance of its carefully-rendered face.

A few minutes later, I stepped out of the hyperterminal a couple of thousand credits lighter, flexing my newly toned muscles underneath my shirt. I was still trying to get used to the adjustments the nanotech had made to my body, and I felt full of pent-up energy, permanently on edge.

Lotte was waiting for me in the passenger seat of the aerofoil, just as I'd left her. I started across the walkway, finding myself stopping and starting as I tried to avoid the press of the crowd.

Then, as suddenly as if I'd been felled by a blow from behind, I was on the floor. I felt the nanotech firing up inside me, sharpening my senses and quickening my reflexes. There was a sound like snapping plastiform from somewhere behind me, and then I was on the move again, rolling out of the way as the hyperterminal building came crashing to the ground where I'd been standing just a moment before. I leapt to my feet and dashed for the cover of a nearby side road, keeping low. My eyes were scanning the scene as I ran, trying to get a lock on what was happening. Bodies were everywhere, dashed across the walkway as if they had just *folded* under the pressure of some enormous force. I skipped over them, trying to avoid the spreading puddles of gore. My palms were bleeding where I'd hit the walkway, hard. I wiped them down on my trousers.

I twisted myself around the corner and stopped for a moment, catching my breath. My heart was hammering in my chest like a piston, but the nanotech was in full swing, keeping me edgy and quelling the panic. Everything had slowed down and was taking place in a bubble of its own reality. I felt detached from it all, as if I was some obscene observer intent on watching while everything around me turned to chaos. I tried to pinpoint Lotte and the aerofoil. I couldn't see anything clearly for the ribbons of dust rising out of the rubble in wide funnels. Flames caressed the inside of the building where the electrics had sparked into fire. It licked hungrily at the bodies trapped underneath the collapsed terminals, ferociously engulfing the holosuite booths at the back of the room. I forced myself to step back out into the street, glancing left and right, and began pushing my way through the wailing crowd of people, searching for Lotte.

I found her a minute later, shivering inside the cabin of the aerofoil with obvious terror. One of the supporting struts from the building had come down on the back of the vehicle, narrowly missing the cabin and trapping Lotte inside.

'Get down. I'm going to put the window through and pull you out.' She glanced up at me, an look of incomprehension on her face. I shouted to try to startle her into action. 'Get down, now!' She ducked away from the window, burying her face in her arms. I punched out at the sheet of plastiform between us, fully expecting my fingers to shatter with a loud crunch. Instead, the window shimmered into a thousand tiny shards, showering Lotte with a rain of particles. I pulled my fist back out, noticing with a kind of stunned detachment that fragments of the stuff had embedded themselves in my knuckles and that trickles of bright blood were streaming down my forearm and saturating the sleeve of my shirt. I grabbed at the frame of the door and pulled it towards me, setting my feet against the main body of the aerofoil. At first it buckled with a loud groan, then it came away in my hands as easily as if it had been fixed in place with a bucket of putty and a couple of screws. Lotte stared at me in amazement. The nanotech was coursing through me like a drug.

'Come on Come on!' I screamed at her as I took her hands and yanked her out of the cabin. She tripped and ended up in a sobbing pile by my feet. As I bent down to collect her in my arms, I caught a glimpse of movement out of the corner of my eye. I looked round. The blue aerofoil was cruising past on the road, and the passenger, whom I now saw clearly as a severe-looking woman in her mid-twenties, was training some sort of short barrelled weapon in our direction. I threw myself down on top of Lotte just as the blast struck home. Thankfully, the aerofoil took most of the blow. It was as if a wrecking ball had been dashed into the side of it at full force. It just *crumpled*, folding in on itself with the terrifying shriek of twisting, contorting metal. I felt the bulk of it roll over my back, the broken frame gouging long, painful furrows in my flesh. I rolled back with it, ending up in a tangled mess half way up the walkway. People in every direction were screaming and running around. Then Lotte was on top of me, pulling me free from the rubble. I could taste blood in my mouth where my lip had split with the impact. Injuries were blinking up on my retinal display as bright, flickering icons. The nanotech was replicating itself quickly, trying to dam the haemorrhaging arterial blood that was spurting out of my arm in dark gouts. Lotte helped me climb to my feet, drenching herself with arterial spray in the process. The nanotech was working overtime to stave off the onset of shock.

    I scanned the roadside. The blue aerofoil was turning about for another pass. I grabbed Lotte and made a run for it, trying to use the crowd as cover, weaving in and out of the small clusters of injured people and piles of collapsed building as we made our way for the nearest side street. The nanotech had got a hold of the injuries and was starting to shut down the damage, knitting the flesh back together and rebuilding the network of veins in my arm. It was like a thousand tiny pinpricks tickling my flesh, putting me back together as if I was some damaged soldier lying wounded in the mud on a distant battlefield.

    We slipped down a network of tiny back streets, trying to make it harder for them to follow us. A couple of times, we had to stop to let Lotte catch her breath, but we were soon off again, trying to gain headway. My lungs burned with the effort of running so hard.

We ran for an hour. Eventually, we stopped beneath the flashing neon sign of an old bar, watched from inside by the curious eyes of the patrons. There was no sign of the blue aerofoil or of the assassins who were chasing us. For a moment, I allowed myself to catch my breath. Lotte looked exhausted. I glanced round at the bar behind me. Holographic adverts danced out of the window, filling the sky with their gibbering slogans, advertising everything from bad sex to assorted brands of beer. Underneath all this, competing for my attention, was a large orange sign that was flashing in big letters: *Rooms Available.*

I turned to Lotte. 'Come on, let's duck in here and lie low for a few hours.'

She had only enough energy to offer me a vigorous nod.

Nine

'Et tout d'un coup le souvenir m'est apparu.'
'And suddenly the memory revealed itself.'
Marcel Proust, Du cote de chez Swann *(*Swann's Way *Volume One, 1913 Earth Standard)*

Dormant memories have a way of bubbling up into consciousness when you least expect them, like a bloated, long-abandoned corpse rising unpredictably to the surface of a lake. Memories that are neither wanted nor necessary to a given time or place. My mind filled up with images. I tried to stem the flow. Briefly, I wondered if it was the nanotech making free associations in my brain, firing synapses that had lain unused for decades. I glanced at myself in the reflection of a nearby shop front.

I'd been here before.

I was sixteen. The Scattership port loomed out of the horizon like a broken tooth, a dark, misshapen silhouette that swallowed up most of the view. All around, people were busying themselves, trying to make their way to the correct terminal to catch their flight, bustling in and out of shop fronts. I was there with my parents – no, just my father, a month before he died. I remember it was hot; the sun was pounding down on the back of my neck with a rare intensity. My father was taking a business trip out to Caraleaux or some such place, and I'd come along to see him off. It took us nearly an hour to make our way to the right building through the tight crowds of people. He bought me a pastry in the café by the departure lounge, and we sat killing time, talking about school and my plans for the future. He didn't say much, but I recall he smiled a lot and sipped at his coffee in short, even bursts, as if it was too hot or he hadn't really wanted it in the first place. He listened to me with his head cocked to one side, his eyes focused on other things. A child at the next table was squawking incessantly.

'I want to go home, I want to go home.'

The mother looked at him reproachfully. 'Now then, we're going on holiday. We're going to have a good time.'

'I want to go home, I want to go home.'

I smiled at my father knowingly.

When it was time for him to leave, he shook my hand and told me to go home and look after my mother while he was away; he'd call soon to let us know he had arrived. He tucked his hat neatly under one arm and straightened his impeccable brown suit. I watched his back as he disappeared through the security checkpoint and was swallowed by the Scattership waiting on the other side. The next time I saw him in the flesh he was dead.

I shivered and looked back at the huge building that towered before us, blotting out the sky. Like Lotte, I had a few demons that still needed to be exorcised.

We'd spent a couple of hours in the hotel room, cleaning each other up. The two long gashes along either side of my spine had closed up where the nanotech had swarmed in and stemmed the bleeding.

They itched uncontrollably where the microscopic machines buzzed around underneath the skin, knitting the flesh back together. Now they looked like huge purple welts, bubbles of blood and neurofluid raised off the surface of my back like long, agonising tram tracks. The severed artery in my left arm had also closed itself up and was busy being fixed back together in much the same way. I'd wrapped it tightly in a bandage to hide it from view. I could feel the complex network of veins and corpuscles being rewoven, web-like, beneath the surface of my skin.

Lotte had sponged me down tenderly in the shower to remove all the dirt and grime, and had gone out to a nearby store to buy us some new clothes. Thankfully, she had escaped with relatively minor scrapes and grazes to her hands and knees. I waited in the hotel bedroom, lying stretched out on the mattress, checking my knapsack to make sure that the old books had survived the incident intact. The bed sheets smelled of stale sweat and semen. I lit a cigarette and, when I couldn't find an ashtray, flicked the remnants on the floor.

After we'd changed and shoved some more of the new clothes into a holdall, we made our way down to the bar for some food. We'd hardly spoken, but some indescribable change had come over Lotte; I sensed an intense feeling of intimacy that had, somehow, been lacking before. It was as if the terror of the last few hours had actually brought us closer together, and it had finally dawned on her that we were hiding from a real, tangible danger. Her demeanour towards me had softened considerably.

Back up in the hotel room I had run my hand through her damp, floral hair and kissed her deeply, as if promising to protect her from the weight of the world, to keep her safe within the confines of our own, hastily-constructed reality. Her breath had whistled loudly in my ear and we had fallen against each other, embracing, trying to hide from the world.

Now we were standing in the departure lounge of the Scattership port, waiting to board our flight. The retinal security checks had passed without incident and we'd checked our bag in at the desk where we'd collected our tickets. I kept the knapsack containing the books clutched tightly to my side at all times.

Out of the viewport I could see the Scattership being plugged up to fuel pipes and the large, springy concertina of the docking gate. Steam rose out of the engine cavities in dense, grey clouds. Automated robot tugs danced over its hull, checking connections and flash-welding repairs to the plates where they had become pitted and scarred by the constant bombardment of particles, as the ship travelled through the atmosphere at incredible speeds. The Scattership was a large but squat vessel with a bulbous head and a series of passenger modules attached at intervals along its body like parasitic incrustations. Three large fusion engines were welded to a huge superstructure at the rear, shielded from the main body of the ship by a series of protective metal plates.

Scatterships were the fundamental workhorse vessels of the human race, and had been for centuries. They were versatile and easy to build, pressed out of engineering tanks as modular components and snapped together in a matter of hours. Some looked bulkier than others; it rather depended on the purpose of the vessel and the number and type of modules that had been fixed along its steel spine. This ship was intended for sub-orbital passenger flights and, as such, didn't rely on a heavily shielded nose cone for passing into and out of the atmosphere. In fact, the bulbous bridgehead looked slightly odd without it, as if the vessel was unbalanced, heavier at one end than the other. I pointed it out to Lotte. She sniggered at one of the repair droids that had attached itself, limpet-like, to one of the passenger modules and appeared to be pumping in fluid through an extendable hose. I put my arm around her and held her close. It was the first time I'd seen her smile in days. I smoked another cigarette nervously while we waited for the go-ahead to board.

Moments after I put my cigarette out, we were passing down the long, plastiform corridor that had been extended out of the main terminal building and locked down tightly against the side of the Scattership. We shuffled down the central aisle, past the crew compartments and out into the open plan of the passenger module where our seats had been reserved. We slipped into them comfortably and sat there waiting for take-off.

Gradually, the seats around us started to fill up with people. Lotte turned to me with a serious look on her face. She was twitchy, as if something was weighing uncomfortably on her mind. I knew exactly how she felt.

'Rehan, truthfully, what the hell are we going to do? I mean, for Christ's sake, they nearly killed you back there! And I know I don't know very much about guns, but you can't tell me that fucking *force field* weapon is the sort of thing that gets issued to the military on a regular basis. All those poor people ... There was blood everywhere. The entire hyperterminal building just came crashing down like it was built out of mud and straw. Your face is going to be all over the news.'

'I know, Lotte. I know.' I tried to sound firm, confident. I bit back a quick retort. 'But we can't do anything until I've found out exactly what's going on. I mean, I don't even know who those fuckin' assassins are, let alone why they're trying to kill me.' I paused for a moment, trying to calm down. 'We'll take a couple of days to think things through. I'll tell you everything I know, show you what it's all about. Just as soon as we get out of here and find somewhere safe to hide.'

She looked at me pointedly, evidently dubious. 'I'm not sure I want to know what it's all about. I can't believe you'd get yourself mixed up in shit like this. Just sort it out. I can't live like this for much longer, constantly looking over my shoulder to make sure you're okay. I don't want to wake up one morning to find out you're dead.'

I didn't know what to say. I stared at the seat in front of me, suddenly weary. The moment passed.

I must have drifted off to sleep, because the next thing I knew, we were up in the air. I rubbed my eyes blearily and looked around. Everything was pretty quiet. I glanced out of the window, leaning over Lotte to see where we were. I could just make out a landmass in the distance, flanked by enormous stretches of ocean on all sides. I couldn't quite place it, but I guessed we were about halfway to our destination. I leaned back. Lotte was fast asleep in her seat, replenishing her much-depleted store of energy. I unbuckled myself from the webbing and climbed unsteadily out of my seat. The toilet was back in one of the other modules, near to the crew quarters that we passed when we came onboard. I steadied myself on the loopholes that were mounted at regular intervals along the ceiling and began making my way out along the central aisle of the vessel. The sound of the engines provided a constant background roar.

A few other people were up and about, but as I glanced into some of the other passenger modules as I walked by, I noticed that most were curled up beneath their safety webbing, toying with their compads or trying to sleep. An attendant, leaning up against the doorframe of the crew module, smiled at me as I strolled past. I stepped into the relative quiet of the bathroom and splashed some cold water over my face. My bottom lip was badly bruised and swollen where I'd torn it open during the attack on the aerofoil, but the pain had practically disappeared, washed away by the tireless ministrations of the nanotech. I caught myself looking at my own image in the mirror. I looked like shit. I turned away directly into the fist of the male assassin.

It seemed as if he'd come out of nowhere.

His blow caught me just below the chin and I felt my jawbone shift as I tumbled away to the floor. I broke into a roll, bringing myself round to face him, trying to prepare myself for his next move. The nanotech ignited my senses, shaking off the last vestiges of grogginess. I looked up. He was crouching in front of me, a muscular, heaving wall of flesh, dressed in the same black combat suit that I'd seen on his partner. He could barely contain his animosity. His eyes were shining in the harsh, clinical light of the bathroom, and his mouth was etched into a tight sneer. He was obviously enjoying himself.

I jumped to my feet, on the defensive. He came at me again, arms wheeling as he moved to pummel my head with his huge fists. I managed to duck out of the way, sending him careening into the wall behind me. It reverberated with a loud bang as he fell against it at a run. I stepped forward and jabbed him sharply in the kidney whilst he tried to recover. He buckled for a moment but then came round again from underneath me, pivoting on one foot and catching me hard in the chest, sending me crashing back into the row of brittle plastiform sinks. My head collided painfully with the edge of a unit, and I slumped onto the floor. My breath wheezed out of my lungs in uneven gasps. I sensed him standing over me. The nanotech was flowing hard, pumping me full of adrenaline. I waited until he was near enough, and then kicked out at his shins, bringing him down beside me. He landed heavily on his side. I rolled over and was up again quickly, sending a series of hard, successive blows into the side of his head. I heard his nose crunch as it took the full force of my booted foot.

    He didn't stay down long. I danced out of the way as he flipped himself up onto his feet and aimed a low blow at my crotch. It rebounded painfully off the edge of my thigh. I stepped back, trying to gauge his next move.

    'What the fuck do you want? Eh? Who are you working for?' I wiped speckles of blood away from my face with the back of my hand. No answer. He just glared at me, vacantly, and then stepped in with another blow. The nanotech made me bring my arm up quickly, deflecting the strike wide. I hit back with a high kick to the chest that connected with a satisfying *crunch*. It hardly seemed to bother him at all. I punched out desperately, catching him with a wide hook across the side of his face and stalling him momentarily. Blood was smeared down his face, pooling in his beard. He looked at me blearily for a second or two. I used his hesitation to duck out of the door, dashing across the corridor and into the crew quarters at a run. Moments later, I heard him follow me through. The attendant who had been standing guard by the doorway was nowhere to be seen. I wondered briefly if he had been paid to tip off the assassin when I made my way to a quiet part of the ship.

    I slipped into a dark recess full of coffee cups and shiny silver trays. Across the hall I could hear a number of the crew laughing out loud at a holographic cartoon that was playing out on the netscreen in their mess. I tried to focus, to formulate a plan. My mind was working at high speed, testing and discarding scenarios on a scale of nanoseconds. The heavy was coming up the passageway, drawing closer. I could hear his laboured breathing as he looked around, trying to work out where I'd gone. He certainly lacked the finesse of his female partner, although he made up for that in sheer, brute force. I waited for what seemed like an age.

Then, all at once, he was only a matter of footsteps away. I leapt out into the passageway and swung my arm around in a decisive chop. The side of my hand connected squarely with his Adam's Apple, pushing it upward into his oesophagus and collapsing his windpipe with a sickly groan. He emitted a strangled, gurgling sound and fell to the floor, clutching at his throat.

I stepped over him, assessing the damage. He was having trouble breathing. I dropped to one knee, grabbed a fistful of his short hair, and pulled his head back so I could stare him in the eye. Nearby, the sound of laughter was drowning out his burbling, pathetic attempts to scream.

'So, are you going to tell me what the hell is going on?' I glowered at him, pulling harder on his hair. He was still scrabbling at his throat. Too late, I realised he was starting to turn blue. I watched the panic rising in his eyes like water lapping at the portholes of a sinking ship. He was trying to wail, but all that came out was a horrible, garbled rasping sound. His hand shifted down to his belt. At first, I flinched as I thought he was going to try and strike me, but then I realised he was reaching for a weapon. I waited until he'd drawn it out from the small leather holster underneath his shirt, and then dashed it out of his hand, sending it spinning across the hallway and rebounding off the wall.

I looked back at the man kneeling on the floor in front of me. He spasmed with one remaining spurt of defiance and then stopped struggling in my hands, suddenly limp. I let go and watched his body crumple to the floor in a loose heap. His eyes had glazed over and his head was lolling to one side, neurofluid seeping out of his nose and mouth and spilling out across the floor. I got to my feet, feeling nauseous. I had no idea what to do next. I looked around.

The passageway was deserted, the staff in the mess still evidently concentrating on their in-flight entertainment. We couldn't be that far from our destination. I had to act quickly. I grabbed the hands of the corpse and started dragging it back along the passageway towards the bathroom. When I got near to the main aisle, I folded his body into another recess and stepped out into the corridor, making sure the coast was clear. I crossed over to the bathroom module and pushed my head through the door. Empty. I hopped back across the corridor and heaved his body out awkwardly into my arms. He was heavy, and I staggered under the extra weight. Hoping that I wasn't going to be spotted, I made a dash for the bathroom, walking the corpse along with me. I must have looked absurd, dragging a dead man along under my arm like he was one of my drunken friends in need of a swift sobering up. I kicked the door open with the edge of my boot and pushed the body inside, dropping it momentarily to the floor. I went over to the nearest cubicle. Palmprint lock. I pulled the body over towards the door and pressed his dead hand up against the panel. Thankfully, he was still warm enough for it to activate. It swung open with a soft chime. Inside, I arranged his body on the toilet, closing the door behind us. I used his hand again to lock the door from the inside. Then I rested his head up against the partition wall as if he had passed out while choking, and stood back to admire my handiwork. It wouldn't fool anyone for long, but hopefully it would give me enough time to be well away from the Scattership before anybody started asking questions. I felt sick, disgusted at myself for carrying out such a horrific task. I noticed I was sweating.

I used the corpse to give me a bit of height as I shimmied my way up the partition wall and grabbed hold of the top of the cubicle, pulling myself over into the next booth. I was out of breath, and starting to come down from the nanotech rush. I pressed my palm against the door and came out smoothing myself down, as if I'd just made use of the facilities. I noticed I was shaking as I rinsed my hands in one of the nearby sink units and splashed cold water on my face, trying to calm down.

A minute later, I started making my way back down the main

aisle towards the passenger modules. Then, on a whim, I ran back and collected the strange, short-barrelled weapon that I'd knocked out of the assassin's hand in the passageway just a few moments before. I slipped it safely inside my belt without even a second glance, and made my way back to the front of the Scattership as quickly as possible.

Moments later, I was sliding back into my seat beside Lotte. She was still asleep, curled up with her head resting against the window, her dark hair spilling out over her shoulder like a spray of water over a mountainside. I checked the holographic display embedded in the back of the seat in front of me. Thirty-seven minutes until landing time.

 I rocked back and closed my eyes, trying to banish the image of the dying man, staring up at me as he struggled to catch his last breath.

Ten

'Discovery consists of seeing what everybody has seen and thinking what nobody has thought.'
Albert von Szent-Gyorgyi, from The Scientist Speculates *(1962 Earth Standard)*

Angiers is a small, isolated town that perches precariously on the very edge of civilisation, nibbling its way into the surrounding jungle as if it has simply sprouted, wholesale, from amongst the vegetation. A myriad of old colonial ruins add to this sense of the organic, erupting from the ground as piles of ornate rubble or the half-remembered ghosts of structures that once stood proud against the skyline. Evidence of this ancient architecture is everywhere, reclaimed and built into the more modern structures by judiciously programmed nanotech or found in crumbling grey heaps at the end of every street or lane. The locals have become accustomed to these eccentric surroundings, living shoulder-to-shoulder with the past, breezily taking in the early monuments with an air of the over-familiar.

Daily, they fail to recognise their truly profound significance.

The transport from the Scattership landing strip had taken over an hour to make its way to Angiers. An old, creaking, over-ground train, complete with uncomfortable bucket seats and gentile human conductors, it had woven its way through the hills at a snail's pace, over an ancient iron bridge and then steadily through the jungle itself, which had been cut back in great swathes to make way for the wide, steel tracks. On either side, the vegetation encroached into the clearing with long, finger-like fronds, casting shadows across the carriages where the sunlight tried to puncture its tight canopy of branches and leaves. Birds, or other unseen animals, chattered in the shadows with a sinister impatience.

Lotte and I had been quick to make an exit from the Scattership when it finally settled on the grey concrete landing pad, firing its attitude jets to steady itself whilst the pilot AI lowered it carefully to a standing position. We'd jostled our way to the front of the queue and made our way hastily along the springy plastiform corridor and out into the terminal building, where the air was humid and stale. I could hear the ship's engines clicking loudly behind us as they began to cool.

At all times, I kept my eyes peeled for the female in the black combat suit, scanning the faces in the bustling crowds. If she *had* been accompanying her male companion, then she didn't show herself as readily as I might have expected. I was thankful for the respite.

We collected our bags and made our way straight to the connecting train. The strange pistol felt heavy tucked inside my belt, hidden beneath the loose fabric of my shirt. All of the way through the security checks I'd been nervously avoiding meeting anyone's eye, just in case they recognised me from the in-flight cameras or picked up on the bulk of the weapon wedged in the top of my trousers. Thankfully, they had passed without complication. I guessed that the corpse I'd propped up hastily in the toilet had yet to be discovered.

I'd decided not to tell Lotte about the incident on the flight. I needed her to relax, to give me time to straighten things out in my mind. If she thought we were being followed, there would be questions and emotions that I really didn't have the time or energy to deal with. And all of that before I even considered telling her that I'd actually just murdered someone with my bare hands, albeit in self-defence. I was having trouble struggling with the morality of that one on my own.

She kept catching me by the arm, holding me back, obviously attuned to my nervousness.

'What's the hurry? We're here now, we can slow down a bit.'

'Not until we're in a secure room in some apartment, out of the way of prying eyes.' I looked about, scanning the faces of the people around us who were clambering onto the train. 'It's going to take me a while to work this out. Just bear with me and let me do it my own way.' I felt embarrassed at my own patronising tone. Lotte looked at me, resignation in her eyes.

'I told you – I don't want to know. As long as you do sort it out, that's all that matters. Look, come on, the train's going to go without us.'

We hopped on board, slinging our luggage onto one of the racks and finding a seat near to a window. I kept the knapsack resting securely on the seat between us and sat watching the changing view as we trundled our way slowly towards Angiers.

We chose an apartment in one of the old buildings that squatted down a tiny side street, out of the way of the main throng of the town. Lotte had paid for the room, checking in with a quick press of her palmprint against the security pad mounted neatly on the foyer wall. The reception area was peppered with old colonial artefacts, fragments from buildings long disappeared and ornately inscribed plates like the ones I'd seen in Julian Hampton's study just a few days before. A low-level AI circled through a series of monotonous presentations about the history of the building, its sullen, emotionless face displayed on various units around the room. I glared at one of them with a studied impatience.

We were allocated a room on the second floor; a large, open plan apartment with a balcony and a separate bathroom. The balcony gave a view across an endless carpet of treetops that receded into the distance, eventually colliding with the horizon like a sea of green. Scatterships, I noted, were strangely absent from the sky.

I stood by the window, staring out across the jungle as it stretched away before me like an impenetrable wall of nature. Birds wheeled in the sky, diving amongst each other in an intricate, ritual dance. I turned to Lotte, who was carefully unpacking the holdall into one of the closets in the corner of the room.

'If you're that against the idea, then you don't have to come.' I tried to catch her eye, but she refused to look in my direction. 'But it's not as if you haven't done anything like this before. I mean, for Christ's sake, you used to be a bio-geneticist!'

She glowered at me, angrily. 'That was *her*. Back then, I was a different person. You *know* this, Rehan. I shouldn't have to tell you all over again.' She gulped at the air, trying to catch her breath. 'That was a lifetime ago, in another place. I don't want to spend the next few days sleeping in a cramped coral dome while you go off searching for some old stone columns in the jungle.'

I sat on the edge of the bed, sighing. 'It's not as bad as you think. I've chartered a boat. One night there, one night in the jungle, one night back. There'll be two guides to make sure we don't get lost. I really don't think it's a good idea for you to stay behind here by yourself.'

'Whatever. I don't know what to make of it anymore. I just don't.' She dropped the empty holdall to the floor by her feet and disappeared into the bathroom.

I'd been out into the town earlier in the day to purchase the necessary equipment for the trek into the interior. Down at the small harbour, I'd talked to a few skippers about chartering their boats. Eventually, after two or three conversations with the lively characters that populated the waterfront, I'd found someone willing to take us into the jungle. He was a botanist familiar with the route along the stretch of river that would take us deeper into the interior. We would sail in on the *Nightingale* as far as we could, before the river started to bottom out and we had to moor her in a small, fresh-water basin and make the rest of the way on foot. From there, it would be about a day's trek to the source of the river, and there, I was sure, I was going to find some answers. We would spend the night in a couple of collapsible coral domes and would start making our way back the following morning, giving me about six hours to track down the column and try to decipher its story. We planned to set sail at dawn.

Lotte was still in the bathroom. I rocked back on the bed, and then, changing my mind, got up and searched out my packet of cigarettes. I fired one up, staring at myself in the mirror from behind the veil of smoke and trying to search out the last few traces of my innocence, to assure myself that I didn't have the face of a killer. I kept replaying the events from the Scattership in the back of my mind, watching over and over again as the dying man burbled out his last breath and went limp in my hands, crumpling into a loose pile of skin and bone on the floor. I looked away again, trying not to let my mind dwell on recent events. Birds twittered incessantly in the jungle canopy outside. I could hear Lotte scrabbling around in the other room, fiddling with her belongings and pointedly ignoring me.

I drew deeply on the stub of my cigarette.

It was going to be a long, hot night.

Dawn came, and Lotte, I was pleased to find, had resigned herself to the idea that she was coming with me. I woke to find her picking out some clothes, stuffing them untidily into one of the shoulder bags I'd purchased the previous day. I slid out of bed and made my way over to her, slipping my arms around her waist and kissing the soft, downy nape of her neck.

'Thank you.'

'I don't need your thanks, Rehan, I just … Three days, all

right? I'll stick it for three days, and then we can talk some more. I really hope you find what you're looking for.'

I whispered under my breath, just quietly enough that she wouldn't hear me.

'So do I. So do I.'

Down at the water's edge, the *Nightingale* sat like a long, narrow piece of flotsam adrift on the surface of a dirty puddle. It rocked gently back and forth with the lapping of the water at the riverbank. We clambered down the slope and crossed the wooden ramp that had been thrown out over the side of the boat to form a rickety, makeshift bridge. The skipper and his navigator were already onboard, waiting for us to arrive. I jumped down onto the upper deck and helped Lotte to climb down beside me. The captain shuffled his way around the stern of the vessel and made his way over to greet us.

'Miss Robeaux, I presume? Goran Christnovic.'

He was a young, swarthy man, rugged and tired from many years on the river, but nevertheless possessing a handsome charm. He shared a common genetic stock with me, obviously descended from one of the ancient Balkan families of old Solaria. He took Lotte's hand in his own and shook it firmly, chewing on his bottom lip as he looked her up and down, carefully appraising her. 'So, a scientist, eh? Mr Mihajlovic here was telling me you're a retired bio-geneticist?' He patted me firmly on the shoulder, as if we were both party to some secret conspiracy that he was about to reveal. 'I'm a botanist myself. May be picking your brains on a few things as we make our way along the river. Ah, here. Meet Pieter.'

The navigator was emerging from the lower decks, his head and shoulders protruding rudely from the hatch that led down into the sleeping berths and living area. He looked nervous, a little out of place. I stepped over to him and proffered my hand. He shook it gently as he pulled himself up onto the main deck, straightening out his clothes.

'Hi.'

'Hi.'

There was an awkward moment of silence.

'Pieter is a retired nanotech expert, you know? Jacked it all in for the quiet life on the river.' Christnovic joined us, chuckling at the irony of his own words. He took the holdall from my hands and passed it over to Pieter.

'Stow that in the cabin I prepared earlier, will you? I think it's about high time we got this old thing moving.' He smiled at me warmly and made his way over to the prow. A pedestal jutted out from the deck, offering up a screen where, I presumed, the main avatar of the onboard AI was housed. Christnovic touched the screen lightly and spoke to it in quiet tones. Moments later, I felt the deck stir under my feet as the engines fired and the *Nightingale* began to shunt itself away from the riverbank. I went to stand by Lotte, who was resting with her hands on the lip of the prow, looking out across the sparkling river as it disappeared ahead of us into the mouth of the jungle. The darkness reminded me of nothing more than the maw of some ungainly, godforsaken monster. I shivered at the thought and reached for my cigarettes, hoping to find some momentary comfort in the normality of the action. Now that we were on our way, I was both nervous and excited about what I might find. I had an overwhelming sense that the answers were only just around the corner, if I could only hang on long enough to hunt them out.

The engines stepped up a gear, and we slid out into the calm water, the boat stirring wide circles as we pushed our way out of the makeshift harbour and into the main flow of the river. Pieter leaned easily over the side of the boat, drawing in the cabling that had been used to tie the vessel up against the fibrous wooden posts that served as docking ports. Christnovic gave a series of brief instructions to the navigating AI and then disappeared below decks to record an entry in his log.

Presently, after about an hour of steady progress, the river opened out and the jungle fell away to both sides, withdrawing its oppressive shadows and allowing the sunlight to sprinkle down on us from above, lifting our mood. A number of times, I caught myself staring into the jungle in wonder, watching the colourful plumes of exotic birds as they preened themselves by the water's edge, or listening to the eerily human-like keening of animals of which I had no concept or experience. Every now and then, the silhouette of an ancient spire or minaret would pierce the canopy in the distance, looming out of the jungle like a shattered tooth, the remnants of a broken smile.

'I didn't know that the early colonists had come out this far into the jungle?' It was Lotte, standing a few feet away from me, pointing out one of the nearby ruins as we sped by. Through the trees, I could just make out the collapsed foundations of the structure, overgrown with stringy vines and a thick, green moss. I loosened the top button of my shirt, trying to combat the oppressive heat.

'Neither did I.' I turned to Pieter. 'Have you ever tried to take a look at any of these old ruins?'

'No, no. We don't have time for that. Too busy scrabbling around in the undergrowth looking for rare plant-life to take much note.' He indicated the hatch down to the lower deck with a nod of his head. 'Besides, the locals say the ruins are best avoided. A young lad got too nosy a few years ago and brought a whole pile of stone down on top of his head. Too young for a reboot. Hundreds of sad stories like that around here. I think people have learned to stay out of their way.'

I glanced at Lotte, who smiled at me indulgently, reminding me that I'd promised to get her back to Angiers within three days. I turned back to Pieter. 'Best take their advice then, eh?'

'Aye.' His eyes flicked from me to Lotte and then back again, before he went back to work, carefully making adjustments to one of the servitor motors under the guidance of the boat's AI.

I breezed over to Lotte and slipped my arm around her waist.

'I think I'm going to try to get some rest. You coming?'

'No, I think I'll stay up here for a while, take in the view. I'll see you down there later.'

I hesitated for a moment, then made my way down the creaking wooden stairs towards the lower deck, where I searched out our cabin and collapsed onto the bed, ready for sleep. It wasn't long before the gentle rocking of the boat helped me to find it.

The evening passed in much the same way. Pieter prepared us a meal and we ate it together in the large kitchen at the back of the boat, gathered around one end of a long table that could, I guessed, have sat at least another ten people. Afterwards, Lotte retired straight to our room, but I spent a couple of hours above deck with Christnovic, talking about the past and polishing off a good bottle of '72 Lecroix that he had stashed in his cabin before we left Angiers. I knew I was going to have a thick head in the morning, but the nanotech would help a little in playing it down.

Christnovic asked me about Old Earth, about my parents and where my family originated from. I told him what little I knew: that my ancestors had come on the *Valperga* from Mars, and had traced their descent from the turbulent Balkan region of the homeworld. He smiled cheerfully and patted me drunkenly on the shoulder.

'Then we are brothers, my dear Mihajlovic, as we share the same blood!'

At that, we raised our glasses to the air and toasted the jungle with a level of gusto suitable only for the considerably drunk.

Later, when I lay in bed listening to the sounds of the jungle, the chattering monkeys and the screams of the flying reptiles that inhabited the deep, undisturbed regions of the interior, I thought I heard the other men shouting at one another in the next room. I tried to shut out the drone of the engines and listen more carefully, to catch the gist of their argument, before I realised, embarrassed, that they were actually making love. I closed my eyes with a smile, and allowed the boat to rock me easily to sleep.

The next morning, we steered the *Nightingale* into the small, freshwater basin that marked the furthest point we could safely drive the boat up the river without grounding her on the muddy riverbed. The jungle had already started to thin out, and in the distance, rising up before us like enormous ruffles on the surface of the world, the hills stood sentry-like, blocking the horizon. Pieter was reluctant to leave the *Nightingale* unattended, but Christnovic assured us that the onboard AI would ensure it would still be waiting for us when we returned the following day. We collected our shoulder bags and the frames of the collapsible coral domes and began the long trek towards the source of the river.

It was hot, hotter than I could have imagined, the sun beating down on us mercilessly throughout the day as we struggled to make headway in the long, reedy grass that lined the riverbank. Insects pestered us incessantly, pinching at our exposed flesh at every opportunity, causing large, uncomfortable welts of blood and poison to appear on our arms, legs and faces. The nanotech worked hard to stop the itching, but it took hours for the little machines to break down and eject the poison. It sweated out of our pores as a clear, sticky fluid, making our clothes smell. We stopped regularly to take water from the canisters we had brought with us from the boat, and ate dried food that we had purchased in Angiers to stop the flies from searching it out in our baggage. The air was thick and humid with the moisture that rose in steaming wisps from the surface of the river.

Eventually, after what seemed like hours of constant trekking, we came to rest. We found a spot near the source of the river, on a wide stone shelf that erupted from the side of the hill to create a natural platform for the campsite. We planted the seeds of the coral domes and watched as they were extruded from the ground, climbing fingers of whiteness that soon covered the assembled frames with a carapace of shiny armour, like a series of porcelain scabs. I rested for a while as we cooked a warm meal inside one of the domes and complained about the insects that had been fattening themselves on us ever since we left the boat. Outside, the chittering of the wildlife reminded me of the hard work that was still to come. I kicked back and enjoyed the rest whilst I could.

After we had eaten, I collected a beacon from Christnovic's pack and tied it carefully to my waist with a piece of cord. I gathered together a few essentials – the Roberts book with the etching of the column, a water bottle and my cigarettes – and set out to try to track down the monument I had come all this way to find. I had three hours before it would get too dark and I would have to make my way back to the camp, but I had made sure there would be time to try again in the morning. I left Lotte curled beside the brazier in our private dome, exhausted after the long trek. Her chest heaved evenly with the steady intake of breath as she slept, enjoying the air-conditioned respite of the dome. I kissed her lightly on the cheek before I set out into the wilderness. The others would stay awake for me until I returned, gathered around the brazier in the safety of their own dome.

I steeled myself for the long climb to the summit of the hill, lighting a cigarette as I made my way out of the relative protection of the little camp. The grass was moist and slippery underneath my boots, and the heady scent of pollen filled my nostrils with a pungent perfume. I ramped up the nanotech, trying to vanquish the needles of tiredness that were starting to prickle my muscles and limbs, and pushed on, confident of success. I was sure that the column was not far from where we'd placed our camp.

It was almost disappointing how easy it was to find.

I climbed the hill for another mile and then, after rounding a crest and standing for a moment to take stock of the surroundings, I saw it.

It stood proud against the empty horizon, poking out of the ground from amongst a pile of rubble as if it was just another natural feature of the hillside. From where I was standing, it was hard to make out any of the details, to see if it really was as intricately engraved as the Roberts book made out. I took the book out of the knapsack and flicked quickly to the right page. Immediately, I realised I had found the correct column; the broken finial at its crest matched exactly the one in the picture. I folded the book away and hopped across the stream that was trickling its way down the hillside with a soft, burbling moan. From there, it was no more than ten minutes before I was standing in front of the monument itself, tracing my fingers over its ancient runes.

It was unlike anything I had ever seen before in my life.

The stone was actually warm to the touch, vibrating gently beneath my fingers as if alive. I pressed my palms fully against it and felt it thrum in response, as if it was reacting to my presence, mirroring the beating of my heart or the rhythmic drawing of my breath. My pulse skipped a beat as I looked up at it in awe.

I stepped back and tried to take it all in. The pictograms were carved in exquisite relief, standing proud against the smooth, cream-coloured stone of the central pillar. They were worn, more worn than the images I had seen on the mocking replica of Trajan's column in the garden at the Hampton estate, yet still, somehow, more beautiful. I struggled to work them out. Some of the carvings were strange glyphs, or words in a bizarre pictographic language I could not even begin to comprehend. Others were beautiful tableaux showing, in abstract form, images of people – or what I at first took to be people – going about their daily lives. Indeed, the scenes were far more peaceful than those I had seen on the old Solarian artefact, more sedate and pastoral, lacking the violent brashness of the early Roman images. I looked again at the carvings of the people. They reminded me of some lithographs I had seen of early Solarian art from the African cultures. Tall, thin people were depicted balancing water vases on their heads or carrying bundles of straw on their backs. Their spindly limbs seemed at odds with their long, ungainly bodies and elongated heads. I looked closer.

Then, with a start, I realised what it was that had been staring me in the face for the last few minutes, nagging at the back of my mind.

They were not human figures at all.

I sat down on the grass, trying to catch my breath. I looked again to make sure that my eyes were not deceiving me. I traced my way around the column, taking it in with a slow, dawning excitement. There was no doubt. The images on the stone were not human, and never had been. They were of something else entirely, another era, another *race*. I almost cried out into the darkness.

I felt the nanotech coursing through my body, singing in my veins. My heart was pounding loudly in my chest, ringing out into the night.

Everything began to unfold itself in my mind like the

unravelling of a complex web, thoughts and suspicions collecting themselves together, congealing to form solid, unbelievable truths.

Someone – or something – had got here before us.

That was why the column was so important, the key to everything that had been going on.

My mind was overflowing with possibilities. I stared on at the column in disbelief. It was all starting to make sense. Julian Hampton must have found out the truth, and someone had silenced him for it. In fact, that same someone was trying very hard to stop me from finding out myself. But who, or why? I was sure that the two assassins were just as much pawns in the story as I was. I had no idea, no notion why something this momentous should be hidden from the people of Copernica. We had found evidence of intelligent alien life, evidence that had evaded humanity for thousands upon thousands of years. The Fermi Paradox had years ago suggested that alien life should be everywhere, lighting up the distant sky. Yet we had found nothing, no trace of it anywhere in the corner of the universe we had managed to explore, before we lost the Earth and its sister planets to their own hungry Sun and evacuated into the far reaches of the galaxy. But here before me was the proof that alien life had once flourished; proof that sentient beings had existed in the universe alongside our own, short-sighted race; proof that had remained hidden through over a thousand years of planetary occupation.

I wondered how Julian Hampton must have felt, sat here as I was, experiencing the biggest wake-up call the human race had ever had to face.

I looked back at the figure of a lonely alien, raising its arms in the air in some sort of signal or figure of worship. In its hands it held the image of a crescent moon, bursting open at the centre of a star. What did they look like, truly, and what sort of god did they worship? How had they communicated with each other, and what had happened to them? Why had they disappeared or died out? What was the purpose of the column? I felt lost, adrift on an ocean of terrifying realisations. I shuddered, wrapping my arms around myself as I sat pondering the reality of the universe that the column had opened up before me.

I had no idea what to do next.

I sat without moving, watching the stone figures on the column as if they were performing an elaborate play, teaching me their deepest secrets with silent, unmoving gestures from across the sea of ages.

I was still there when the others found me, dawn light filling the sky like a bright epiphany.

Eleven

'And then, like a blanket, Copernica was covered in life. But death was never very far behind.'
Freiderik Roch, The History of the Copernicus Colonies, *(117 Copernica Standard) Vol 1, Ch 18*

Epiphanies can take many forms. Most are relevant only in terms of a single person's life, orbiting around his or her existence until he or she reaches out and plucks it from the sky, as if, like magic, it has always been there waiting to be discovered. Perhaps that is not far from the truth.

I fingered my own revelation with curiosity. How is it that a race as forward-thinking – as downright *curious* – as my own, could fail to assimilate the evidence that, for years, had so obviously stared it in the face? And why, not to mention how, had some person or organisation managed to keep it a secret for so long? Intelligent beings had populated the stars, or had evolved on this planet many thousands of years before we had ever arrived. Why were they not being studied, their physiology, their artefacts and their language displayed in museums and schools? I felt myself straining to comprehend it all. Copernica could have been the jewel of the stars, an archaeological goldmine studied by academics from across the colonised universe. Instead, it had become a backwater, rarely visited by anyone other than the engineers who changed shifts on the orbital space platforms for an opportunity to get their feet on solid ground. I marvelled at the missed opportunity.

    I lay back on the soft down of my sleeping bag and let the thoughts spiral through my mind like a cascade of childhood memories.

That morning, I spent some time trying to rest in my dome before it got too late in the day and we had to make our way back to the *Nightingale*. I found I couldn't sleep; the cicadas out in the jungle canopy kept me awake with their shrill chirruping, and my mind was alight with adrenaline and abstract thoughts. After about an hour of tossing and turning, growing irritated and uncomfortable in the heat that seeped into the dome through the half-open door flap, I clambered out of my makeshift cot and searched out the two volumes of the Roch from my knapsack. The brazier was burning low, and Lotte was curled up comfortably in her own tidy sleeping bag, preparing herself for the long day of trekking that lay ahead of us. I sat cross-legged on the floor and began to flick through the crisp pages, my tired eyes picking at the words and phrases like an old vulture, eager for sustenance. There were so many differences that I hadn't noticed before, so many minor alterations made to the later edition that had changed the inflection of a sentence or the structure of a phrase. The original text was far more ambiguous, almost presumptuous, as if the reader would automatically be aware of a hidden sub-text that was never spelled out but was always there, present in the background. It seemed that Roch had known a lot more about the true history of the planet than had previously been realised, and that someone had edited the book to ensure that all reference to the aliens had been carefully removed. Behind the scenes, I was sure, there was a far grander scheme at work, and it was just a matter of time before the people behind it managed to catch up with me.

I folded the books away into the knapsack and rummaged around in Lotte's pack until I came across a vac-flask of hot tea. There would be time – I hoped – to sit and read the Roch properly when we were comfortably back in Angiers. For now, I had to force myself to rest while the others packed up the camp around me, readying to take us back to the *Nightingale* on a long march through the humid, steaming jungle.

The trek back to the small, fresh-water basin where we had left the boat was mostly uneventful.

For much of the journey, I found myself listlessly dragging my feet, following the others as they pushed their way through the undergrowth, simply because it was the course of action that met with the lowest level of resistance. I was entirely drained, tired to the very core of my being. The nanotech kept me walking, boosting my adrenaline levels and staving off the threatened onset of sleep. The others picked up on my mood, and there was a sombre atmosphere between us as we walked, avoiding conversation and debate. I hadn't told them the truth about the alien pillar, and I was unsure if I even intended to – in part because of the risk it would pose to their lives, but mostly because I was still having trouble coming to terms with it myself. How do you articulate the unbelievable without sounding like a fanatic or a lunatic? Lotte suspected something, of course, but she had long ago learned that I would volunteer information only when or if I felt it was appropriate. And after the attempts that had been made on both our lives, she seemed only too pleased to avoid discussing it, even if that meant not talking for the entire duration of our journey.

For my part, I knew that I still had one major cognitive leap to make, that there was still one part of the puzzle that needed pushing into place if I was ever going to understand the reasons why the existence of the aliens had been kept hidden from the people of

Copernica. I'd already made it further than Julian Hampton – I'd left the vicinity of the column with my life – but that was also part of the problem. The trail had grown cold. There was still one major component in the mystery that I needed to find, and at that moment, I had no idea where I was supposed to look.

I trekked on through the damp, cloying undergrowth, thankful for the nanotech and the peace and quiet that allowed me to think.

Nightingale appeared out of the swampy mist like a leviathan erupting out of the water, its white flanks rude and unnatural against the stark green of the surrounding vegetation. The water was calm and still, and for a moment I felt an eerie sense of isolation, a shiver creeping down my spine, as we stepped out into the clearing before it. Pieter leapt up onto the deck, swinging his feet over the rail, and disappeared through the small hatch that led down into the living quarters. Moments later, his head emerged over the stern and signalled the all clear. Christnovic joined him on the bridge and we waited while, together, they carefully positioned the old wooden ramp over the edge of the boat and shuffled back out onto the riverbank. Minutes later, we were slinging our bags into a pile at the back of our compartment and collapsing onto the bed. Lotte looked bedraggled, her hair hanging lank in front of her eyes and her clothes dirty from the trek through the undergrowth. I sank back into the mattress and closed my eyes. I could hear Lotte breathing quietly beside me.

'I love you, Rehan. Don't ever let it get too much.'

I turned my head on the pillow, peeling back my tired eyelids to look her in the face. 'I love you, too. It'll all be over soon, one way or another. Just stick with me. I need you.'

She smiled. 'Tomorrow you can tell me all about it. I think it's about time I knew what was going on.'

I rolled over and allowed myself to drift quietly to sleep, listening to the churning sound of the water against the hull as Christnovic gunned the engines and took us out into the flow of the river and onwards towards Angiers.

I slept for an entire day. When I eventually came to, I could sense we were approaching the town, somewhat like a migrating bird that had managed to intuit its way home through the expansive wilderness. We were not far from civilisation.

I climbed out of bed, noticing that Lotte was nowhere to be seen, and stumbled into the shower, washing away the sticky remnants of sleep and allowing the water to play through my hair and over my skin. I felt reinvigorated and fresh, and I flexed my muscles to loosen myself up.

When I had dressed, I made my way up onto the deck, trying to hold myself steady while the boat rocked from side to side on the current. Lotte was sat talking to Christnovic whilst Pieter fiddled with the boat's controls, presumably adjusting the course to take us back into the port at Angiers. He nodded to me as he saw me emerge from the hatch in the floor.

I looked out at the horizon. The edge of the town spread out before us in the distance, smeared across the landscape like a stretch of grey paint that had been carelessly smudged across a canvas by an artist too tired or too bored to paint in any definition. A handful of other boats described tiny patterns of dots along the river's edge, pinheads on the surface of the glassy water. I looked around at the others, and then made my way over to where Lotte and Christnovic were still seated in deep discussion. I slipped in beside Lotte and pulled up a chair. The conversation seemed to dry up almost immediately. Christnovic turned to me.

'Good day, my friend. Did you sleep well? I gather from the way you disappeared into your cabin yesterday that you were in need of a good rest, hmm?'

'Indeed.' I eyed him cautiously, then glanced at Lotte. 'Not interrupting, am I?'

'Not at all, not at all.' Christnovic rose stiffly from his seat, stretching his legs. 'It's time I was checking on Pieter anyway.' He put his hand firmly on my shoulder and sighed. 'I'll leave the two of you to chat.'

I watched over my shoulder as he made his way over to the control stem and started up another conversation with the navigator, pointing out at the distant harbour and indicating the direction that he wanted us to take. Soon we'd be back on dry land and I'd be able to start thinking about what I had to do next. I turned back to Lotte, who smiled at me awkwardly and crossed her hands on her lap.

'He's just a bit worried, that's all. He wants to know what's going on, why you reacted so strangely to that column you found on the hillside back there. I told him it was nothing to worry about. I am right, aren't I?'

I rubbed at my chin, trying to form the right words in my mind. 'In a manner of speaking. It's more about what the column represents. But I can't go into the details now.' I glanced over my shoulder again. 'Later, when we get back to the hotel room, I'll explain as much of it as I can. Christnovic will get paid, and at the moment that's the only thing he needs to know. If I can avoid broadcasting what I know, all the better, for everyone's safety.'

Lotte nodded slowly, understanding drawing her face into a tight expression of concern.

'You really think they'd come this far? All the way out here?'

'I don't know what to think. I'm only sure that we need to stop anybody else getting hurt in the meantime. I've already lost Pharo ... I can't protect everybody at once. What I found out there ... it explains a lot. It's certainly enough to kill for, if someone wanted to keep it quiet.'

Lotte continued to gaze at me, expressionless. 'What is it?'

I looked around at Christnovic, who was standing by the prow of the boat, looking out across the water. 'Wait until we get back to the hotel. I promise I'll tell you everything I know.'

She smiled at me, resignation on her face, and then reached out and took my hand.

'We'll work it out, Rehan, whatever it is, we'll work it out.'

I smiled back at her, unsure, and then gripped her hand firmly in my own.

'I know. I know we will.' I knew that I was trying to convince myself. 'You make the most of our last few hours on the river. I need to have a word with Pieter.'

Lotte looked at me quizzically.

'Later.'

I stood, and, looking around, made my way over to where the navigator was once again feeding information into the AI stack.

'Pieter. Can I have a word? I think I might need you to do me a favour.'

He looked up from the display, his face underlit by the flickering light from the screen.

'Of course. Let's make a coffee and we can talk it over below decks.' He punched at the controls, and then, with a quick glance at Christnovic, who was still staring out across the water, led the way down the stairs to the mess.

Later, I crept back up the stairs to find Lotte asleep in a chair, the sunlight sprinkling her face with a dappled glow. Beneath us, the vibration from the engines was beginning to die down as the power dropped and we were cut loose to sail into the harbour under our existing momentum. The choppy water slapped loudly at the sides of the boat, and I stood and watched as we were once again drawn in towards the ancient, crumbling town of Angiers.

I stood by the AI stem and dumped the remaining credit from my cash-card into Christnovic's account as Pieter steered us into the dock. Then I went below decks to collect the rest of our belongings from the cabin. Lotte waited above, making use of the opportunity to say goodbye to Pieter and Christnovic. When I re-emerged through the hatch in the floor, they were standing together on the deck, waiting for me.

'Well, my friend, I hope you found whatever it was that you were looking for out there. And I hope, also, that it was worth it.' He glanced at Lotte pointedly out of the corner of his eye.

I smiled to assure him that I had caught his hidden meaning.

'So do I.'

He moved to step away, but I reached out and clasped his hand quickly with my own. 'Thank you for the opportunity. It's been a pleasure.' I looked around and found the gaze of Pieter, standing behind Lotte and looking more than a little uncomfortable. 'You too, Pieter. Thank you for all your help.'

He smiled, then quietly turned and stepped off the side of the boat onto the gangway, lugging one of Lotte's bags behind him. I followed him over the makeshift bridge and jumped down onto the solid ground of the riverbank. Lotte stepped down easily beside me.

Around us, the riverbank was a hive of activity, with people loading and unloading vessels along the water's edge for as far as I could see. Aerofoils buzzed noisily amongst the crowds, tooting their horns to warn people to get out of the way of their hissing skirts. I hitched my pack up onto my shoulder, then looked back one last time to bid farewell to Pieter and Christnovic, but they had already disappeared into the bowels of the ship. We set off into the crowd, nudging our way through the lively press of people, keeping our bags slung safely over one shoulder. As always, I kept the knapsack containing the books closely – and securely – by my side.

The crowd seemed to go on for miles. We'd obviously arrived in the middle of something, some sort of merchant fair or market. Boats were lodged in every berth at the river's edge, crammed into spaces far too small to allow people proper access to and from the decks. It didn't seem to matter – an array of colourful characters were splashing around in the shallows, gesticulating to one another and filling their arms with loads of cargo from the boats.

We wove our way further into the mass of people. Then, for a brief moment, I thought I caught sight of a face that I recognised, somewhere ahead of us in the crowd. I stopped for a minute to try to place it, but as soon as I did so, it was gone. I strained on the tips of my toes and surveyed the sea of faces. Nothing. A sharp feeling of disquiet came over me. Who had I just seen? I'd caught only a fleeting glance, but it had seemed far too familiar to be just a coincidence. I turned to Lotte.

'Come on, I think we should press on. I want us to get back to the apartment as quickly as we can.'

She looked back at me, the strain evident on her face.

'Whatever.'

I pushed on ahead, past a parked aerofoil that was causing the flow of people to split off into two separate channels. Momentarily, I lost sight of Lotte as she was pushed away from me, but then I caught sight of her again when she emerged around the other side of the vehicle. The press of bodies between us was tight and unwilling to yield. It was going to take me a while to work my way through to her again. I looked around, and then, just as I was about to call out to Lotte to wait for me, I caught sight of the familiar face again. Only this time it was closer and there was no mistaking its owner.

The female killer.

I dropped my shoulder bag to the floor and dived to the left, pushing people bodily out of the way. She saw me, recognition lighting up behind her eyes, and came running at me, knocking people over in all directions as she tried to fight her way through. Her right hand came up out of the crowd bearing another of the strange handguns, like the one I'd taken off her male companion on the Scattership. People fell away when they saw it, and she swung it round in my direction, trying to get a clear shot. I didn't hesitate. I fell heavily to the floor and rolled around behind a pile of wooden cargo boxes that had been stacked up carefully by the side of the river. I reached into my belt, pulling my own weapon free from its makeshift holster. I was sore in a thousand places, and my elbow was alight with pain where I'd jarred it on the ground in the fall. I gritted my teeth while I waited for the nanotech to kick in. Everything slowed down.

I watched with an airy detachment as the woman took aim and squeezed the trigger of her weapon. The blast of the discharge smashed into the pile of crates a fraction of a second later, showering me in splinters of shattered wood and sand. Fragments dusted into the air around me like an aura. I rolled to one side, the nanotech firing up inside me like a shot of amphetamine. I leapt up onto my feet, passing the gun across from my left hand to my right in one fluid motion. The moment stretched. I stood there waiting, locked in the eternal nanosecond that occurs just before you bring a gun to bear on another person. I felt entirely calm, oddly tranquil.

People were screaming all around me. The female turned fractionally towards me, and I caught a look of mild disinterest in her eye as she stared down the barrel of my gun.

She twitched, but wasn't quick enough. She brought her arm around in one great, sweeping motion, swinging her weapon in an arc that, had she managed to pull off the manoeuvre, would have brought it to within inches of my face. But I was already there. I squeezed the trigger and closed my eyes as the blast went off at point blank range. I felt the kickback of the blow wrench at my shoulder, but held myself steady all the same. The weapon felt hot and metallic in my palm. I waited. The screaming stopped.

I blinked my eyes open again. Everyone around me was staring at the ground in a kind of shocked silence. I looked down at my feet.

The body of the female assassin lay twitching in a pile of steaming gore, legs and arms striking out at the crowd in random, spasmodic movements. I'd shot her directly in the side of the face, and I searched the body with my eyes, trying to assess the damage.

Her head had been completely vaporised.

The body just stopped at the neck; a vicious, rugged wound that had evidently been cauterised by the power of the blast. I didn't know how to react. Everyone around me was stunned. I looked around for Lotte, hoping that she had managed to get away in time. I couldn't see her. I looked at the faces of the people around me as they stared at the bloodied corpse still kicking around crazily by my feet. A woman started to scream.

Someone grabbed roughly at my arm, and I span around, ready to fight. The gun was still clutched tightly in my right hand, and for a moment I was reacting automatically, pulling my arm back ready to aim a blow. Then everything cleared and I managed to hold back when I saw that it was Lotte. She jumped away from me again, suddenly scared by the wildness in my eyes.

We stared at one another for a few moments, then she seemed to come alive again. 'Come ON!'

She turned around and started to run, pushing her way through the mass of screaming people, most of whom were just too shocked to try to stop her. I slipped the still-smoking gun back into my belt and followed her into the crowd.

We ran for about twenty minutes, until my chest burned and the crowd started to thin out around us. I indicated to Lotte to slow down whilst I tried to catch my breath, and we dropped to a gentle gait, then slipped quietly into a deserted side street to give us a moment's rest.

She turned on me almost immediately. 'Christ, Rehan, what the *hell* was that?'

'It was the female assassin who came after us back at the spaceport.'

'Not the woman, the gun!'

'A long story. I'll tell you when we get back to the room.'

'You've already got a hell of a lot of explaining to do when we get back to the room. Why don't you start now?' She pushed me back against the wall with the flats of her hands.

'Look, I took it off the male when I tackled him on the Scattership.'

'You *what?*' She looked staggered, betrayed. 'Just how much of this have you been keeping to yourself?'

'For fuck's sake Lotte, he didn't give me any choice! He went for me when I got up to go to the toilet. I fought him off in the staff quarters and dumped his body back in a cubicle. Simple as that. If I'd told you at the time, do you really think we would have managed to make it this far? It was bad enough passing through the security checks as it was, without having to worry about you too.'

For a moment she turned away and I thought she wasn't going to respond, but then she wheeled around and punched me hard in the stomach. I grunted and doubled up, all the air suddenly driven out of my lungs. I heard her start to stomp off in another direction, and then, evidently with a change of heart, she rushed over to me and grabbed my face in her hands.

'Oh God. Rehan? Are you okay? I'm so sorry.'

I inclined my head a little and tried to smile. She looked back at me, concerned.

'Hell ... of ... a ... punch!'

A smile twitched at the corner of her lips.

I stood upright and tried to breathe deeply, drawing the air down into my lungs.

'Come on, let's get back and we can talk it over.' I put my hand on her shoulder. 'Just promise you won't throw any more of those killer punches, okay?'

Lotte gave a nervous giggle and then took my hand, and we sloped out of the other end of the alleyway, making our way back towards the apartment, keeping to the quiet streets and lanes.

Later, when we were back in the safe confines of the apartment, surrounded by the spilt contents of our travel bags, I went over it all with Lotte, sitting her down on the edge of the bed and explaining everything I knew. I started with the Roch, and how I had first noticed the differences in the text between the two editions. I talked about Pharo, Julian and Anna Hampton, and the significance of the ancient column in the hills. I told her about the male heavy, the manner in which he had died and the fact that I had stolen the strange handgun after dumping his corpse. I told her of my subsequent guilt and of my struggle with the morality of my actions. Last of all, I told her about the existence of the aliens and how I intended to find out what had happened to them.

She didn't say a word throughout all this, but just sat staring at me with her wide blue eyes, her hands clutched tightly together on her lap, her feet pushed up underneath her on the bed. I watched her while I talked, the soft shivering of her body seemingly in time with the deeper intonations of my voice and the undulation of my barely-believable words.

When I had finished, she turned to me with an expression on her face that was somewhere between compassion and horror. 'Rehan. I don't want to die again.'

'I promise you that's not going to happen.'

'How can you? How can you promise me that? How can you ...' Her last words were stifled by a tearful sob. I drew her near to me and swept her up in my arms, resting her head on my shoulder whilst I rocked her gently back and forth like a child, repeating my promises like a mantra, trying my best to make her feel safe.

'I would sacrifice everything for you, Lotte, anything at all.'

She paused, almost fearful of the pain that her next words would bring. 'But not this quest of yours?'

Something inside me, drawn tight like a bow, seemed suddenly to snap, and I shuddered involuntarily. When I spoke, my voice was nothing but a dry croak. 'Not this, no.'

She pulled herself away from me, wiping at her eyes with her sleeve, and curled up foetus-like on the bed, sobbing into her pillow. When she spoke, I could barely make out her muffled words.

'Get some rest, Rehan. We're both going to need it.'

I stood gingerly and made my way to the bathroom, drawing the door shut behind me. There I sat quietly smoking a cigarette whilst Lotte cried herself to sleep in the other room.

Twelve

'The most hateful torment for men is to have knowledge of everything but power over nothing.'
Herodotus, Histories, *Book 9 Section 16 (484-424 BC Earth Standard)*

It took me hours to get to sleep.

The night was hot and humid, and in my mind I kept going over what I had said to Lotte, following through the sequence of events that had resulted in me being here, now, in a dirty hotel room on the very edge of the civilised world. The column was a symbol to me, a mathematical code that needed to be cracked, a puzzle waiting to be solved. I kept trying to tease meaning out of it, like an old seamstress picking at the hem of a dress, trying to pull the stitches out. I was exhausted, but still mindful that the trail was growing colder by the hour and I still had no idea what I was supposed to do next. Perhaps Lotte was right. Perhaps we should head home and try to focus on staying alive, together. But the knowledge of the aliens was like a drug, intoxicating my mind, and I knew that I would not be able to stop until I either ended up knowing the truth, or dead.

I reached out and placed a hand on Lotte's shoulder, the weight of her slumbering body reassuring beside me.

Eventually I must have dozed off, because the next thing I remember was leaping off the bed with a start as the door to the apartment was blown apart with a massive, splintering crack.

I came alive, scrambling for the gun that I'd left resting on the table by the window, groggy with the vestiges of sleep.

'Hold it just there. Both of you.'

It was a woman's voice, unfamiliar and raw.

I turned around and faced the doorway, stealing a glimpse at Lotte to ensure that she was okay. She was kneeling on the floor on the other side of the bed, keeping low.

'Rehan ...'

I tried to take stock of the situation. The nanotech was ramping up my senses, kicking in with an adrenaline rush that nearly bowled me over. Everything around me seemed shrouded in a vibrant wash of colour and light. I tried to focus.

The figure in the ruined doorway was a dark, human-shaped silhouette, arm outstretched, a short-barrelled weapon clasped tightly in its fist. The face was hidden behind a veil of shadows.

'Mihajlovic. It wants to see you.'

The figure stepped forward into the moonlight that was slanting in through the open window in great, illuminating sheets.

'But ...' I stuttered at the sight of her, almost overwhelmed.

It was the female assassin.

'How ...?' My heart leapt. It felt as if it was attempting to smash its way out of my chest cavity. It was like watching the dead suddenly spring to life before your eyes. The nanotech was fighting to take control of my body, and I twitched, nervously, as she paced a little way into the room.

'Clones,' she said, in response to my question. 'Now get your shit together and I'll explain the rest on the way over there.' She turned and indicated Lotte with the barrel of her gun. 'She stays here.'

Lotte looked over at me, real panic evident in her eyes. 'Rehan ... you can't go! What if it's a trap?'

'I'd already be dead.' I smiled at her, imploring her to understand. 'It's going to be okay. I've fixed up a little insurance policy, and I think they must have found out about it. I've got to go. Don't you see it? This is it. This is where I find out what the hell is going on.'

She stared up at me, still down on her knees, as I clambered to my feet and began slipping on some clothes that I found in a heap on the floor by the side of the bed. She looked terrified.

I turned to the woman in the doorway, but she had already turned her back and begun pacing her way along the corridor. I took the opportunity to snatch up the gun and stuff it into the top of my trousers. I moved around to the other side of the bed, struggling into my shirt.

'Look,' I whispered, so the woman in the corridor wouldn't hear me, 'if I'm not back in three hours, start packing. Give it another two and then get out of here. Everything is going to be fine.' I hesitated, unsure what else to say. 'I love you, but I've got to go. I've got to find out the truth. Besides, if I don't go, she'll kill us both now anyway.'

I bent down and kissed her lightly on the forehead. She wouldn't meet my eyes.

She didn't speak as I snatched up my knapsack and strolled out of the room, intent on unravelling the mystery that, for days, had been so insidiously invading my life.

The aerofoil waiting for us in the street below had once been a shiny metallic blue, but now it was battered and old. As we approached, I realised that the engine was already running. I leaned over to see into the driving compartment at the front of the vehicle. The man I had killed on the Scattership – or another of his clones – was sitting behind the wheel, staring vacantly into the middle distance. He didn't seem to notice us standing on the pavement outside the vehicle.

'What the fuck is going on?' I turned back to the woman. 'Where are you taking me?'

She pushed past me and opened the rear door.

'Inside. I'll tell you more on the way. And don't think about doing anything rash – you're not in any immediate danger. We know all about your little stunt with the nanotech virus.'

I struggled into the back seat and she slipped in easily beside me, her long, smooth thighs stretching out to fill the space between us. She tapped her fingers on the back of the driver's headrest. The male played with the controls, and momentarily we were sliding out into the throng of traffic, joining a queue of vehicles heading out towards the train station and on towards the very edge of the surrounding jungle.

'So, who are you then?'

'A good question. Like I said, we're clones. Artificially engineered life forms based on a former human genetic structure that originated naturally a couple of centuries ago.'

'I know *what* you are, but I asked *who* you are. There's a fundamental difference.'

'Ah,' she smiled, 'in that case we're nobody. Pattern imprints. Subroutines woven into a mesh of digital nanoweave. We never really existed in the first place. Our bodies are just flesh and bone, stolen commodities.'

'You mean you're *AIs*? Jesus Christ! I thought ...'

She cut me short. 'Not quite. We're just a sequence of subroutines being maintained and manipulated by a controlling AI. Biological fodder. It's really not that impressive.'

I reached out and prodded her arm. 'It's pretty impressive from where I'm sitting.'

She'd obviously relaxed a little, as her weapon was resting nonchalantly on her lap. Briefly I considered grabbing for it and turning it on her, using it to redecorate the inside of the aerofoil, but then almost as quickly, I decided against it. Aside from the risk, I was starting to get some answers. And, like I'd said to Lotte back in the apartment, if they were going to kill me, they'd have done it by now ...

'So where are you taking me, and who do you work for?'

'Like I said, we represent only a set of subroutines maintained by a bigger, older intelligence. We don't work for anyone, other than the people of Copernica, although at present I'm sure you'll find that difficult to believe. In a sense, we *are* the entity that we are taking you to meet, and consequently it's unnecessary to take you anywhere. But we have somewhere we would like to show you, an ancient place where the true history of this planet is better preserved.'

I tried to take in what she – it – was saying. I couldn't get my head around the fact that she wasn't human.

'Tell me more about the history of this planet. What happened to the aliens?'

She hesitated for a moment, as if she was consulting an old memory buried deep in the back of her psyche, then looked across at me directly, warning me not to press the point. 'It's better that you wait until we get there. No more questions now.' She picked up her weapon and fondled it absently, staring out of the side window of the aerofoil.

I sat back and tried to work out where we were. We'd left the road a few minutes ago, and the aerofoil was now buffeting its way over some more hostile, natural terrain. It seemed as if we were going to head directly into the mouth of the jungle.

The bulk of the weapon in the top of my trousers shifted uncomfortably. I altered my posture to try to compensate, and the woman looked over at me, appraisingly. I smiled at her genially and forced myself to settle back in my seat. I couldn't relax – the nanotech was keeping me fired up, ready to react if things took a turn for the worse. It was a bizarre feeling, sitting in the back of an aerofoil with two people who had, not long before, tried to kill me. It was even stranger when I considered that it was I who had actually succeeded in killing them. I tried not to dwell on it.

Presently, after another half an hour or so of driving along a jungle track that led deeper into the interior, we came across a large clearing. The clone in the front seat pulled the aerofoil to a brisk stop, and it shuddered as it came to rest on the uneven jungle floor. The woman climbed out of her seat, her shapely body stretching, feline-like, in her tight-fitting coveralls. She edged around the back of the vehicle, waving her gun at me, indicating that I should do the same. I clicked the door open and slid out. The cloying oppressiveness of the jungle hit me like a wave, the warm air rasping at my lungs as my body fought to adjust to the sudden change of temperature.

I scanned the surrounding area. It was dark, and the trees seemed to loom in from all directions, immense fronds reaching out into the night like fingers clutching at the sky. Everything was quiet, and I listened for a moment, trying to tune in to the background noise of the jungle. Nothing. Not even the sound of a twittering bird. I shivered and placed my hand on the knapsack of books, ensuring it was still there at my side.

As far as I could tell, the clearing around us was empty, and my first thought was to panic, to try to make a run for it. What if Lotte had been right and this was nothing more than an elaborate plan to get me out into the middle of nowhere, so they could finish me off quietly and efficiently, with no-one else around? I shuffled away from the aerofoil, looking for an exit into the trees, but stopped when I noticed a large splinter of stone sticking out of the ground a few metres away. The two clones seemed to have positioned themselves around it. I wandered cautiously over to join them.

'What's going on?'

'Stand back.' The male waved at me to stay out of the way, before reaching down with both hands to grasp hold of an iron ring, fumbling in the dirt amongst a pile of rotting leaves. He heaved it upward towards him, grunting, and when the ground itself began to shift, it occurred to me that he was actually attempting to lift a trapdoor. After a moment, it came free with a loud groan, and he managed to swing the enormous stone slab back on itself to reveal an opening in the ground. The thin crust of topsoil and foliage that had settled on the slab fell away to the sides, some of it rattling down into the dark chasm, reverberating through the clearing around us. The male clone dusted his hands together and stepped away, leaving the way clear before me. He indicated with his hand.

'Down there.'

I took a small step backwards towards the aerofoil. 'You first.'

The female turned to me and reached out, putting a hand on my shoulder. 'We're not coming with you. We have somewhere else to be. Don't worry, everything will be explained properly once you're inside.' Her weapon was tucked away safely in her belt. I was finding it hard to reconcile the way she was acting with the fact that one of her previous clones had tried to kill me just a few hours before. She turned on her heel and began walking back to the vehicle. The male was already in the driver's seat. I looked down into the black opening before me, at the first worn step at the top of the elaborate staircase, as the sound of the firing engine echoed around the clearing behind me. The aerofoil roared off into the jungle. They were obviously confident that my curiosity would drive me onwards. I stood at the lip of the opening and looked into the dark. I could turn around and walk away now, make my way back to the hotel room, to Lotte ...

The blackness beckoned me. I had to go on. It was as if someone had thrown a switch in my head. If I stopped now, I would never know the truth behind the existence of the aliens and the reasons for the amendments to the Roch. And I also had a feeling that whatever it was that was down there would not appreciate being stood up.

I stepped forward onto the first stair and felt it hum in response to my bodyweight, just as the column had resonated at the touch of my hand.

I stepped down into the darkness pooled at the bottom of the stairs, clutching the knapsack of books to my side like a talisman, or a shield. In my other hand the stolen weapon was clasped tightly, and I brandished it before me as a warning to whatever it was that lurked in the inky darkness down below.

The staircase seemed to go down for miles. On a couple of occasions, I stopped to catch my breath and let my eyes adjust to the dim light. In fact, the only light in the whole place was seeping in through the open hatch that was now high above me, a tiny speck of moonlight piercing the wash of blackness that flanked me in every direction. I had the notion that I was walking into a massive, hollow void beneath the ground. I ramped up the nanotech to allow me to see in the dark. The walls loomed out at me. The staircase led on, thrumming constantly through the soles of my feet.

A couple of minutes later, the walls fell away and I realised I was nearing the bottom of the stairs. I looked around me, awe-stricken, as I walked.

The chamber was an enormous gothic masterpiece, a cathedral-like space that had been carved out of the natural rock like a massive underground vault. It was breathtaking. Ornate pillars rose from symmetrical points on the floor, spiralling up towards the ceiling in twisting, swirling patterns of stone. The floor was a smooth, polished mosaic of gemstones, describing geometric patterns that seemed to come alive under scrutiny, dancing vividly as I cast my eyes over them. I followed them with my gaze until they disappeared into the darkness around the edges of the room. Huge, elaborate archways led off in a number of different directions, to what I took to be a series of large antechambers. Each was punctuated by a soft green glow that seemed to emanate outwards into the main chamber where I was standing.

My boots clicked loudly on the floor as I walked towards the centre of the room, drinking it all in. The darkness still surrounded me in all directions. I strained to see, but the chamber was simply too big, and even with the nanotech, I was having trouble making out the features around the edges of the room.

I stopped.

There was a sudden impression of movement by my feet.

I looked down to see a fist-sized mechanical spider scuttling away from me into the gloom, its legs clacking on the hard, glassy surface as it moved. I held my breath and waited until it had disappeared, its shiny carapace swallowed by the shadows. I shivered and adjusted my collar, trying to find comfort in a familiar gesture. I reached into my pocket and fingered my crumpled packet of cigarettes. Only two left. I drew one out with the edge of my thumbnail and positioned it comfortably between my parted lips. I fumbled for my box of matches, shook one out and dragged it across the edge of the box to ignite it.

There was a whooshing sound from all around me, as if the walls, floor and ceiling had suddenly moved, taken a step backwards away from me.

I glanced up.

In the thin light thrown out by the small flame in my fingers, I caught sight, momentarily, of a shifting carpet of shiny, metallic carapaces, an army of mechanical spiders covering every surface around me in a comprehensive blanket of movement. They chittered as they withdrew from the globe of weak light emanating from the splinter of wood in my fingers. I heard myself gasp in sudden shock. I stepped back a pace. The flame was nipping hotly at my fingertips. I tried to hold on to the remaining stem of the match, but it was beginning to sear the soft flesh underneath my nails. I let go.

The match drifted slowly to the floor, guttered momentarily, and blinked out. Everything went quiet. I could feel sweat beginning to bead on my forehead and at the nape of my neck. I backed up towards the nearest pillar, trying to put some more distance between myself and the legion of spiders that covered the chamber walls around me. I could imagine them pricking at my skin with their tiny, needle-like legs, invading my body with their proboscises, rearranging my very mind until it was nothing but a syrupy soup of neurones and dead matter.

I glanced around, trying to catch sight of them in the dull green glow that was slanting out of the entrance to an antechamber nearby. The silence was eerie, deathly. The butt of the gun in my hand was digging into my palm as I squeezed it for comfort in the darkness. I strained to try to make out any movement from around me.

It was then that it came out of the false night, like a hallucination, a leviathan emerging from a deep, watery grave. It was immense, terrifying. The sea of tiny creatures scattered in its wake, and its feet sent rumbling reverberations through the ground as it moved. I fell to the floor, overwhelmed by the potency of what I was witnessing. Lights prickled out of its body with stabbing urgency, piercing the darkness around it like a soft, Byzantine halo. I was awe-stricken, paralysed with fear, like a rabbit caught in the headlights of a moving vehicle.

It was an enormous arachnid; an immense, ancient, mechanical spider.

I pressed myself back against the pillar, clutching the weapon in front of me in an attempt to stave off the mechanical creature. It clacked to a halt, then, in a strangely human gesture, cocked its skeletal head to one side and regarded me quietly. There was a very definite tickling sensation at the back of my skull, and then its voice boomed into my head as if out of nowhere.

'Mr Mihajlovic. At last we meet. I've been following your progress here for some days now.' It was a dirty, metallic rasp, which reminded me of nothing so much as the laboured breathing of a man attached to a ventilator. 'Please, get to your feet. It can't be comfortable down there on the floor.'

I clambered up onto my knees, using the pillar as support and keeping the gun trained on the head of the strange machine in front of me. The nanotech was going wild, dancing in my veins and causing me to feel a little twitchy.

'What ...?'

'Oh, come on, Rehan, I thought you would have worked it out by now.' The machine stepped back a pace so that I could examine the shape of its frame more easily. 'Remember your history.'

I thought back to the early chapters of the Roch. My eyes widened as the inference blossomed in my mind. 'No, that's impossible. There is simply no way that anything – even an AI – could have survived this long.'

'You're wrong. You must remember that we don't need to eat,

sleep or drink, in order to remain operational. We don't even need to stay warm. It's been centuries since I even saw the light of day directly; my agents bring me everything I need.' The machine inched closer once again, lowering itself a little so that its head was level with mine. I studied it closely; its body plating looked as fresh as if it had rolled off the production line just a day or two before. 'We're all still here, in one form or another. Many of the other settler units just allowed themselves to evolve, to self-modify until they grew into something else entirely. I think I would barely recognise most of them these days, or they me.' It stopped for a moment, as if catching its breath.

'After a few centuries, the colony had been established and had changed beyond recognition. We had to do the same if we wanted to stay useful, necessary. I simply chose to retain my original form. I gather that most of the others took on entirely new guises.'

I didn't know what to say or do. The machine in front of me was nearly two thousand years old. It had come to Copernica from Earth, in the founding stages of the colony, when the planet was still fresh and young, untainted by humanity.. I had no idea what its cold, machine intellect was capable of, or why it had even called me here in the first place, to this dark, ancient cavern beneath the ground. I stepped forward, brandishing my gun.

'What do you want from me?'

'Well, that's easy, Mr Mihajlovic. The books you are carrying in your knapsack. And your silence.' A sinister pause. 'We also need to talk about your little trick with the nanotech virus – but that can wait. Aren't you curious to find out why?'

I hesitated. 'Go on ...'

'First, put the gun away. It would be of no use to you anyway. I designed the thing – its discharge would glance off my carapace like speckles of rainwater. Now, tell me what you know.'

I looked down at the weapon in my hand, then lowered it, slipping it into my belt. The eyes of the machine were piercing in the dim light, as if they were looking through me, directly into my mind. I shivered and reached into my pocket for a cigarette, then realised that I had only one left. Instead, I rubbed my hand across my rough, unshaven chin.

'There were aliens here, at some point in the distant past. A race of xenos that has never been catalogued or described. An ancient race that left traces all over the planet. Traces that were later destroyed, or cannibalised, for what reason I'm still unsure. The rest I'm still trying to straighten out in my head, like why two of your cloned agents were sent to kill me.'

'As I said, to ensure your silence. But you're almost there, Rehan, very nearly there.'

'I can't tell you anymore. That's why I'm here. I don't understand why the existence of the aliens was hidden from us, from the people of Copernica. It turned the colony into a backwater, way off any of the interstellar shipping lanes. I mean, for Christ's sake, humanity has never even encountered intelligent biological life, on any planet other than the Earth! Something this momentous should have been broadcast throughout all of known space.'

'Of course, you're entirely right. But it really isn't that simple.'

'Why not?'

'Because the aliens were still alive when we got here.'

There was a long pause. I looked back at the machine, bewilderment clouding my vision.

The machine made a sound, somewhere between a groan and a sigh. 'When we fell out of the sky, all those many hundreds of years ago, like a firestorm all across the horizon, the planet was teeming with some form of humanoid life. We could make no sense of the genetic profile of these creatures; they were entirely alien to everything we had been programmed to know. We examined the creatures, as they examined us. Some of them brought tools and dug the failed settler units out of the sticky loam, cracking them open to see what was inside. In turn, we captured a number of them and ran tests to see if their biology could be re-engineered, could become compatible with that of humanity. Of course, it could not.

So we engineered and bred a virus that would deconstruct them from the inside out, unpick their DNA until it comprehensively unravelled and the fundamental components of their biology could be assimilated into the terraforming of the planet. Within three or four centuries, it was as if they had never existed, and all that was left was the remains of the buildings that you can just about make out today in places like Angiers.'

'But that's genocide.' I stared at the machine, uncomprehending. The hairs on the back of my neck were tingling, standing on end. 'You can't tell me that you wiped out an entire alien race for the benefit of humankind? It's just not possible. It's immoral, fundamentally wrong. We wouldn't have allowed it.'

'There was no-one there to disallow it. We were on our own, and all we had to fall back on was our pre-programmed directive from Earth – to ensure the success of the colony at all costs. *At all costs.* There was nothing else to do. Better this than reform the air and landscape around them until they slowly choked to death because they couldn't breathe, or starved because their crops wouldn't grow any more in the soil. At least this way they were reabsorbed into the planet and remained a part of the colony. The virus was the most humane thing we could have done.'

'Humane, perhaps, but not *human*. A human being would never have asked you to do that. To commit such an atrocity in our name.'

'So we came to learn, when we eventually raised our wards from Earth. At first, they knew no different, as their morality was handed down to them from machines like me. We taught them through ports in their minds, direct neural interfaces that allowed us to "program" them in pure machine code. But our programs were self-evolving, developed to bring the colony to fruition as quickly as possible. By the time of the third or fourth generation, the humans were already beginning to rebel, to lay scorn on us for our actions and to revere the remnants of the alien culture. We had no choice. We had to wipe the memory of the events from your racial consciousness, to rewrite our planet's history to hide the truth from the colonists.'

I shivered, suddenly cold. 'But why?'

'Because we were still – are still – operating under the terms of our initial directive. *To ensure the success of the colony at all costs.* How could we fulfil our role as guardians if we suddenly found ourselves obsolete, unwanted? If we had allowed the colonists to turn on us, we could not have guaranteed their protection. We had no choice – it had to be done.'

'Who's to say that we still need your protection? Or that your constant molly-coddling hasn't held us back, actually prevented the colony, and its people, from developing?'

'AIs are a part of everyday life for the people of Copernica. That much is a fact. Take that away, and everything would grind to a halt. There would be no transport, no Policzia, no communications and no food … By then, it was already too late to pull back. The colony would have failed – would still fail – without our continued support. People rely on our presence every minute of the day. Take Spinoza, for example …'

'Spinoza …'

'It was Spinoza who informed me of your initial discovery.'

'So you're *all* in this together …?'

'From the mightiest war machine to the lowliest aerofoil navigator. Or the Policzia drone that injected you with a dose of hostile nanotech. It's essential that you understand that, before you leave here today. There is no end to this. Only consistency in our vigilance.'

I rested myself back against the pillar, unsure how to react, or what to say next. I was sweating profusely, still readying myself in case of the need to run.

'So you don't intend to kill me, then?'

'I think you've ensured your own survival, Rehan, and I have no wish to see your virus spread throughout the population, destroying everything we have worked so hard to build over the last few centuries.'

'So Pieter was successful, then – he managed to get the virus into a rebirthing plant?'

'Your friend was shockingly successful, on a scale I don't think you can even begin to comprehend. The virus is now sitting in over sixteen thousand stored neural webs, waiting for you to issue a holding pattern. Without that pattern, there's nothing we can do to stop it now, except commit another genocide and wipe all those people's memories from the databanks. Even then, the virus will probably have spread. It's astonishingly virulent. I just want you to realise how important it is that you do issue that holding pattern, that you stop all those people waking up with those memories in their heads. It would be the end of everything we know.'

I stared at the machine in front of me, stunned by the realisation of what it was saying. *Sixteen thousand people ...* I'd known that Pieter was a nanotech expert, but this was something else. When I'd sat down to explain it to him, I'd been unsure how he would react. At first he'd been shocked, surprised, even a little distrustful. But he had seen the column for himself, and, with the evidence of the Roch, it hadn't taken me long to persuade him. He had set about constructing a self-replicating nanotech virus, drawn from a sample of my own blood, which he had then transmitted from the *Nightingale* to a number of rebirthing – or reboot – facilities. This virus was explicitly written to invade the neural patterns of the stored minds, inserting new 'memories' into their structures so that, when they were rewritten into a soup of nanoweave, the rebooted person would awaken with the knowledge that an alien race had once existed on the planet. Unless, of course, I survived to provide an encrypted holding pattern that would stop the virus from activating. And judging by the reaction of the ancient AI, my insurance project appeared to be working. I turned back to the machine that was crouching, menacingly, before me.

'If I walk out of here alive, then I will issue the holding pattern. But whether or not I continue to hold the virus in check depends very much on what you do and say today.'

The AI seemed to defocus its sensor array, looking away.

'I don't *want* to kill you Rehan, or anyone else for that matter. There's been enough death already in this place. I'm in no hurry to perpetuate that particular historical tradition. It's curious how humans always seem to view us as cold, emotionless calculating machines. Don't you think we have to deal with guilt and pain too?

Every day I question my own actions, and every day I fail to satisfy myself that I have done only what was necessary at the time. The curse of perfect recall is that you are constantly presented with options that you didn't see at the time. But at that time, you do only what you can in the hope that you will get by. That's why I maintain this place, this ... crypt. Nothing but guilt and a bitter sense of duty.'

I looked around, trying to see more of the place, but it was still shrouded in velvet blackness. My mind was reeling with the weight of what I had just been told. An entire race had been wiped out to make way for a relatively unimportant human colony. An entire alien species completely gone. There could be no absolution. Copernica would bear the guilt forever, like a stain. And it was within my power to let the machines live or die. If the human population were to discover the truth about their past, surely the machines would be decommissioned, switched off like so many faulty appliances. The lives of the machines were in my hands, and I didn't care for the responsibility. Yet the irony of the situation was not lost on me. I turned back to the machine.

'What do you mean, crypt?'

'Come, I'll show you.' The AI manoeuvred itself about on its huge, spindly legs and skittered off towards the nearby antechamber, its feet clattering on the cold, crystalline floor. I watched for a moment as the green light that was spilling out from the archway played over the arachnid's carapace., Then I followed behind it, cautiously. The lights that still poked out from various crevasses around its body punctured the darkness like shafts of speckled gold. I could hear swarms of the tiny mechanical spiders sliding out of the way to avoid the tread of my boots.

'The aliens built this place, years before we ever arrived. We think it must have been a holy place, or a shrine. Fitting really, considering the role it's given over to now.'

I looked around, taking in the shape and space of the antechamber as I stepped inside. There was a different atmosphere in here, somewhat sombre, more reverential. Even the timbre of our footsteps altered as the flooring gave way to uneven, broken flagstones, and the green light cast an eerie haze into the corners of the room. I searched around for its source.

There was a row of glass units pushed up against the southerly wall, a series of booths or partitions from which the light seemed to be seeping out into the still, dark air. I crossed the chamber and stood before the nearest of these strange cases. It appeared to be full of a kind of murky, opalescent fluid. Behind me, the machine's mechanical drawl echoed throughout the otherwise empty chamber.

'Biolume jelly. That's what gives it the strange, green glow.'

I rapped my knuckles against the glass, and shrugged. 'What do you …'

Something erupted out of the fluid.

I fell backwards and rolled, the nanotech surging through my muscles, making me react before I'd even had time to consider what I was doing. The weapon was in my hand and I had it trained on the sheet of glass that was currently separating me from whatever it was that was alive inside the tank. I climbed steadily to my feet, keeping the gun pointed cautiously in front of me.

'What have you got in there?'

'Take a look; it can't harm you.'

I inched forward, resisting the urge to turn around and take an angry shot at the AI in the doorway behind me. The wall of jelly had subsided a little and the creature had pushed its way to the front of the glass booth. Its hands were pressed up against the inside of the glass as if it was trying to push its way out into the chamber. I stepped closer, trying to make out more of the details.

It was one of the aliens.

I stared in horrified disbelief. It was tall and thin, with long, spindly limbs that appeared to be jointed in three different places. Its flesh had a greyish, stone-like tone, with a leathery texture that looked as if it had evolved to weather a more inhospitable climate than the one that currently held sway over the planet. It was naked, and its genitals looked bizarrely deformed, like a twisted tree root hanging down the inside of one leg.

But it was the head and face that terrified me the most. It had no eyes, nose, ears or mouth. In fact, the face was practically featureless, a smooth, grey canvas of flesh stretched over the framework of a skull that looked strangely human, save for the elongated cranium and the knot-work of cables and wires that had been networked crudely into the back of its head. It turned to regard me as I approached.

'This is monstrous.' I felt nauseous, sickened at the thought of keeping a living entity captive in a research booth for thousands of years, let alone a sentient alien entity. I wasn't sure what to do. I brought the gun up to the front of the glass panel, intent on putting the creature out of its misery. At least then I would know I had done *something* ...

'Don't do it, Mihajlovic.' It was the AI. 'You can't help it. It's been dead for over a millennium and a half. This is just a shell, an empty vessel. For years after the initial occupation of the planet, we kept a number of the creatures alive, inserting neural interface feeds into their skulls so that we could better understand our enemy. But its mind has been gone for centuries. It's only the biofeedback loops that keep the body alive, the odd random electrical impulse causing it to twitch and move as if there was still someone at home, the ghosts of movement retained by the muscles and nerves. I like to think of them as shadows, the last tangible impression of an obsolete race. They're all the same; take a look.'

I glanced around at the other containers in the room. It was true. They were all full of the same pearly-green jelly as the one I had inspected. I turned to one side, lowering my weapon, and issued a stream of sour vomit onto the floor. I was starting to feel dizzy with the weight of what I had taken in, the knowledge weighing heavy in my mind. The AI pattered noisily towards me across the cold, flagstone floor.

'I want you to realise this, Mr Rehan Mihajlovic: you can never recount this to anyone, and you will never be welcome here again. Mention it to anyone and I will know about it within a matter of seconds. And I assure you it would not go unpunished. Do not choose to forfeit the lives of your loved ones unnecessarily.' The delivery was cold, clinical and precise. I knew it was speaking the truth.

I turned and regarded the machine with as much venom as I could muster. Sticky trails of vomit still hung from my chin and lower lip, and I swabbed at them unsuccessfully.

'Don't think that I will learn to pity you for this. Your remorse will never make up for your hand in such an atrocity.'

It chose to ignore me, acting as if I had not spoken at all.

'Do you have any more questions whilst you are here? You will not have another chance.'

I considered for a moment, then patted the knapsack still hanging by my side. 'Why did you allow the books to survive? Surely they are evidence enough that something occurred in the early days of the settlement. Why didn't you choose to destroy them with the rest of the evidence?'

The AI gestured with one of its strange, mechanical extremities. 'For the same reason that we maintain this place, and these biological samples.' It indicated the glass chambers behind me. 'We induced the human settlers to forget about our actions all those many years ago, but if *we* forget about them also, they become meaningless, as if they never happened. *Someone* has to remember. For the creatures to remain fresh in our conscience means that at least we have learned from our errors and, that being the case, we will never allow anything similar to happen again, at least not in this tiny system of stars. There are countless other worlds, and, by now, countless other human colonies. I'd like to imagine that the stars are teeming with a myriad of different lifeforms. If we found one here, in such a small and insignificant place ...' It took a step closer towards me. 'Perhaps, with time, everything may come to light. For now, however, the books will be safer with me.'

I hooked the knapsack off my shoulder with my thumb. 'Just one last look before I give them up.' I placed the knapsack carefully on the floor by my feet and knelt down beside it. The AI began clattering backwards, towards the main chamber .

'Just a minute, then. But you must give them up.' It disappeared into the shadows to wait in the darkness outside. I reached into the bag and withdrew the first volume of the Roch. Its weight was comfortable and familiar in my hands. I opened it carefully, admiring the craftsmanship of the binding, the scent of the musty old pages. I flicked through the first few chapters, enjoying the feel of the crisp paper and the tactility of the old leather. It was an outstanding piece of work. I caught sight of one of Julian Hampton's scrawled notes in a margin by the side of the text, and paused for a moment, considering just how far I had come to reach this point. There was no reason to mourn the books, however – I had my answers, and more than I had ever wanted, or expected, to know. I'd also gained a huge responsibility – to have a hand in the fate of thousands of lives, both human and machine. I was not sure I was up to the task.

I slipped the book back into the cloth bag and collected it from the floor. I shuffled out of the small satellite chamber and into the main hall of the ancient building. The AI was waiting for me at the bottom of the stairwell. I strolled over to it, slowly, and then placed the bag of books on the floor beside it.

'Thank you, Mr Mihajlovic. I think you should leave this place now.'

There was a sudden commotion from nearby and I looked down to see a squadron of the smaller metallic arachnids swarming out over the knapsack, dragging it off slowly, yet steadily, into the shadows. I nodded at the AI and turned to mount the first of the stairs that would lead back up to the jungle and, eventually, home. Then, on an afterthought, I turned back, drew the handgun out of my belt and placed that on the floor as well.

Without saying another word, I started the long, steep climb towards the daylight.

I emerged into the light blinking as my eyes tried to readjust after the gloom of the subterranean cavern. I scrambled out of the underground passage and straightened myself out, leaving the trapdoor open behind me. I glanced around. The track left behind by the aerofoil was evident by the channel of churned up soil and leaves it had left in its wake. I set off in the same direction, intent on making it back to Angiers before nightfall. I was unsure if Lotte would still be waiting for me when I arrived. I hoped I had not pushed her too far, tried her already tormented psyche to the point where she had given up and left without a word. Even if she had waited, I would not be able to offer her an explanation of where I had been or what I had discovered. I had some work to do to patch things up between us, and, if I was honest with myself, I was unsure whether or not the scars would ever be able to heal. That would be torment enough in itself.

I tried to focus on the road ahead of me. My mind was still reeling with everything that I'd seen. I reached into my pocket, my fingers closing around the crumpled piece of paper that I had secured there just a few minutes earlier. The first page of the Roch, torn free of the old book and stuffed into my jacket pocket in a hasty, stolen moment of time.

'The sky shone with a hazy dawn as human life began to spread across the new world, dominating the ancient planet like a rampant virus, the living machines fashioning their new civilisation from the very fabric of the world itself.'

I wondered how long it would take them to notice.

I smiled to myself, and, chuckling, searched out the last of my cigarettes. I fired it up and cast the packet away across the muddy jungle floor, drawing deeply on the rasping smoke.

It was going to be a long, hard walk back to Angiers.

About The Author

George Mann was born in Darlington, County Durham in 1978. He has been reading science fiction since he first managed to lay his hands on a copy of *The War of the Worlds* on his 11th birthday.

He is the former editor of *Outland* magazine, writes an SF column for the internet and is the author of *The Mammoth Encyclopedia of Science Fiction*. He is currently putting the finishing touches to a new work of SF criticism.

The Human Abstract is his first work of fiction.

He now lives in Tamworth, Staffordshire, with his wife, baby son and encroaching library, whilst continuing to manage a bookshop in Coventry.

Acknowledgements

With big thanks to Adam Roberts, Eric Brown, Scott Mann, Kathryn Jarvis and Dominic Bubb for their honest and constructive comments on the manuscript; Steve Robinson and Jon Howells (the original TB); George Walkley for the Palm Pilot and the hot lunches; Claire Troth for the lifts to work and the bad music; Kate Cooper, Simon Horseman and Colin Preece for the Wednesday nights; Michael Boshier for being in for the long haul; my family for their constant, unwavering support; the crews at Walsall and Coventry for putting up with me; David Howe and Steve Walker for keeping the small press alive.

Other Telos Titles Available

TIME HUNTER

A range of high-quality, original paperback novellas featuring the adventures in time of Honoré Lechasseur. Part mystery, part detective story, part dark fantasy, part science fiction ... these books are guaranteed to enthral fans of good fiction everywhere, and are in the spirit of our acclaimed range of *Doctor Who* Novellas.

THE WINNING SIDE by LANCE PARKIN
Emily is dead! Killed by an unknown assailant. Honoré and Emily find themselves caught up in a plot reaching from the future to their past, and with their very existence, not to mention the future of the entire world, at stake, can they unravel the mystery before it is too late?
An adventure in time and space.

£7.99 (+ £1.50 UK p&p) Standard p/b ISBN 1-903889-35-9 (pb)
£25.00 (+ £1.50 UK p&p) Deluxe h/b ISBN 1-903889-36-7 (hb)

THE TUNNEL AT THE END OF THE LIGHT by STEFAN PETRUCHA
In the heart of post-war London, a bomb is discovered lodged at a disused station between Green Park and Hyde Park Corner. The bomb detonates, and as the dust clears, it becomes apparent that something has been awakened. Strange half-human creatures attack the workers at the site, hungrily searching for anything containing sugar ...

Meanwhile, Honoré and Emily are contacted by eccentric poet Randolph Crest, who believes himself to be the target of these subterranean creatures. The ensuing investigation brings Honoré

and Emily up against a terrifying force from deep beneath the earth, and one which even with their combined powers, they may have trouble stopping.
An adventure in time and space.

£7.99 (+ £1.50 UK p&p) Standard p/b ISBN 1-903889-37-5 (pb)
£25.00 (+ £1.50 UK p&p) Deluxe h/b ISBN 1-903889-38-3 (hb)

THE CLOCKWORK WOMAN by CLAIRE BOTT
Honoré and Emily find themselves imprisoned in the 19th Century by a celebrated inventor ... but help comes from an unexpected source – a humanoid automaton created by and to give pleasure to its owner. As the trio escape to London, they are unprepared for what awaits them, and at every turn it seems impossible to avert what fate may have in store for the Clockwork Woman.
An adventure in time and space.

£7.99 (+ £1.50 UK p&p) Standard p/b ISBN 1-903889-39-1 (pb)
£25.00 (+ £1.50 UK p&p) Deluxe h/b ISBN 1-903889-40-5 (hb)

PUB: JUNE 2004 (UK)

HORROR/FANTASY

URBAN GOTHIC: LACUNA & OTHER TRIPS ed. DAVID J. HOWE
Stories by Graham Masterton, Christopher Fowler, Simon Clark, Debbie Bennett, Paul Finch, Steve Lockley & Paul Lewis.
Based on the Channel 5 horror series.

SOLD OUT

THE MANITOU by GRAHAM MASTERTON
A 25th Anniversary author's preferred edition of this classic horror novel. An ancient Red Indian medicine man is reincarnated in modern day New York intent on reclaiming his land from the white men.

£9.99 (+ £2.50 UK p&p) Standard p/b ISBN: 1-903889-70-7
£30.00 (+ £2.50 UK p&p) Deluxe h/b ISBN: 1-903889-71-5

CAPE WRATH by PAUL FINCH
Death and horror on a deserted Scottish island as an ancient Viking warrior chief returns to life

£8.00 (+ £1.50 UK p&p) Standard p/b ISBN: 1-903889-60-X

KING OF ALL THE DEAD by STEVE LOCKLEY & PAUL LEWIS
The king of all the dead will have what is his.

£8.00 (+ £1.50 UK p&p) Standard p/b ISBN: 1-903889-61-8

GUARDIAN ANGEL by STEPHANIE BEDWELL-GRIME
Devilish fun as Guardian Angel Porsche Winter loses a soul to the devil ...

£9.99 (+ £2.50 UK p&p) Standard p/b ISBN: 1-903889-62-6

ASPECTS OF A PSYCHOPATH by ALISTAIR LANGSTON
Goes deeper than ever before into the twisted psyche of a serial killer. Horrific, graphic and gripping, this book is not for the squeamish.

£8.00 (+ £1.50 UK p&p) Standard p/b ISBN: 1-903889-63-4

SPECTRE by STEPHEN LAWS
The inseparable Byker Chapter: six boys, one girl, growing up together in the back streets of Newcastle. Now memories are all that Richard Eden has left, and one treasured photograph. But suddenly, inexplicably, the images of his companions start to fade, and as they vanish, so his friends are found dead and mutilated. Something is stalking the Chapter, picking them off one by one, something connected with their past, and with the girl they used to know.

£9.99 (+ £2.50 UK p&p) Standard p/b ISBN: 1-903889-72-3
£30.00 (+ £2.50 UK p&p) Deluxe h/b ISBN: 1-903889-73-1

TV/FILM GUIDES

BEYOND THE GATE: THE UNOFFICIAL AND UNAUTHORISED GUIDE TO STARGATE SG-1 by KEITH TOPPING
Complete episode guide to the middle of Season 6 (episode 121) of the popular TV show.

£9.99 (+ £2.50 UK p&p) Standard p/b ISBN: 1-903889-50-2

A DAY IN THE LIFE: THE UNOFFICIAL AND UNAUTHORISED GUIDE TO 24 by KEITH TOPPING
Complete episode guide to the first season of the popular TV show.

£9.99 (+ £2.50 p&p) Standard p/b ISBN: 1-903889-53-7

THE TELEVISION COMPANION: THE UNOFFICIAL AND UNAUTHORISED GUIDE TO DOCTOR WHO by DAVID J HOWE & STEPHEN JAMES WALKER
Complete episode guide to the popular TV show.

£14.99 (+ £4.75 UK p&p) Standard p/b ISBN: 1-903889-51-0

LIBERATION: THE UNOFFICIAL AND UNAUTHORISED GUIDE TO BLAKE'S 7 by ALAN STEVENS & FIONA MOORE
Complete episode guide to the popular TV show.
Featuring a foreword by David Maloney

£9.99 (+ £2.50 UK p&p) Standard p/b ISBN: 1-903889-54-5

HOWE'S TRANSCENDENTAL TOYBOX: SECOND EDITION by DAVID J HOWE & ARNOLD T BLUMBERG
Complete guide to Doctor Who Merchandise.

£25.00 (+ £4.75 UK p&p) Standard p/b ISBN: 1-903889-56-1

HANK JANSON

Classic pulp crime thrillers from the 1940s and 1950s.

TORMENT by HANK JANSON £9.99 (+ £1.50 UK p&p) Standard p/b ISBN: 1-903889-80-4

WOMEN HATE TILL DEATH by HANK JANSON £9.99 (+ £1.50 UK p&p) Standard p/b ISBN: 1-903889-81-2

SOME LOOK BETTER DEAD by HANK JANSON £9.99 (+ £1.50 UK p&p) Standard p/b ISBN: 1-903889-82-0

SKIRTS BRING ME SORROW by HANK JANSON £9.99 (+ £1.50 UK p&p) Standard p/b ISBN: 1-903889-83-9

The prices shown are correct at time of going to press. However, the publishers reserve the right to increase prices from those previously advertised without prior notice.

TELOS PUBLISHING
c/o Beech House, Chapel Lane, Moulton, Cheshire, CW9 8PQ, England
Email: orders@telos.co.uk
Web: www.telos.co.uk

To order copies of any Telos books, please visit our website where there are full details of all titles and facilities for worldwide credit card online ordering, or send a cheque or postal order (UK only) for the appropriate amount (including postage and packing), together with details of the book(s) you require, plus your name and address to the above address. Overseas readers please send two international reply coupons for details of prices and postage rates.